DE

When Templar's sister had a baby by Alex
Marcose and then both she and Alex died,
Templar took the child herself. But
Alex's forbidding brother Leon didn't
know all this, and naturally had the
lowest opinion of Templar—an opinion
that didn't prevent him marrying her for
baby Keri's sake. How could Templar
tell him the truth now—when it would
mean his taking the child away from her?

Books you will enjoy
by CAROLE MORTIMER

SAVAGE INTERLUDE

James St Just was Kate's half-brother, but for
family reasons they wanted the fact kept secret—
with the result that Damien Savage had jumped
to all the wrong conclusions about Kate. And as
in a very short time he had become the only man
in the world for her, she had quite a big problem facing her . . .

THE TEMPESTUOUS FLAME

Caroline hadn't the slightest intention of allowing
her father to marry her off to Greg Fortnum,
whom she didn't even know apart from his
dubious reputation. So she ran off to the wilds
of Cumbria where she met the mysterious André,
who turned out to be an even greater threat to her
peace of mind than her father and Greg Fortnum
combined . . .

TEMPTED BY DESIRE

Vidal Martino was the man of Suzanne's dreams—
tall, dark, handsome, charming and rich!—and he
seemed attracted to her. But her beautiful,
bitchy stepmother Celeste had her eye on him
too. Why couldn't Celeste transfer her attention
to Vidal's even richer brother Cesare and leave
Vidal to Suzanne?

ONLY LOVER

To escape the clutches of a too-demanding
girl-friend, Joel Falcone wanted Farrah to pretend to be his fiancée—and to save her father's
career she was forced to agree. But she found
Joel too disturbingly attractive already; what
would happen when she found herself in even
closer contact with him?

DECEIT OF A PAGAN

BY

CAROLE MORTIMER

MILLS & BOON LIMITED
LONDON W1

All the characters in this book have no existence outside the imagination of the Author, and have no relation whatsoever to anyone bearing the same name or names. They are not even distantly inspired by any individual known or unknown to the Author, and all the incidents are pure invention.

The text of this publication or any part thereof may not be reproduced or transmitted in any form or by any means, electronic or mechanical, including photocopying, recording, storage in an information retrieval system or otherwise, without the written permission of the publisher.

This book is sold subject to the condition that it shall not, by way of trade or otherwise, be lent, resold, hired out or otherwise circulated without the prior consent of the publisher in any form of binding or cover other than that in which it is published and without a similar condition including this condition being imposed on the subsequent purchaser.

First published 1980
Australian copyright 1980
Philippine copyright 1980
This edition 1980

© Carole Mortimer 1980

ISBN 0 263 73251 7

Set in Linotype Plantin 11 on 11½ pt.

Made and printed in Great Britain by
Richard Clay (The Chaucer Press), Ltd., Bungay, Suffolk

CHAPTER ONE

TEMPLAR smiled down tenderly at the tiny infant she had just cradled to sleep, brushing back the fiery curls so like her own auburn tresses. Keri was the most important thing in her life, and for her she would gladly do anything. And if prices continued to rise as they were doing it could just come to that.

She sat down tiredly in the worn leather armchair, her bearing one of dejection and defeat. She just couldn't manage any more. Keri was growing up all the time, and besides the food factor, she was getting too much of a handful for the elderly Mrs Ellis to look after. While she had still been a baby it hadn't been so bad, but now that she was starting to crawl about her little fingers were into everything.

Templar buried her face in her hands, the tears of frustration and defeat coursing unheeded down her pale cheeks. What could she do? Oh, what could she do! If only Tiffany hadn't died giving birth to Keri, they could perhaps have sought help from the baby's father. But she *had* died. And Templar didn't know who Keri's father was. If only she hadn't been working abroad two years ago, none of this would have happened, and perhaps Tiffany would still be alive. If only, if only, *if only*! How many times had she said the same things over and over to herself in the last year? And where did it get her? Nowhere!

She wouldn't give Keri up, no matter what happened. She would rather starve first. She looked up quickly as a loud knock sounded on the door, glancing apprehensively at Keri as she began to stir. It had taken her a long time to get the baby to sleep, and if whoever it was at the door woke her up, she would give them a piece of her mind.

She got wearily to her feet, intending to open the door before her visitor repeated the loud knocking. Keri whimpered as she walked past and she lingered to give her a word of assurance. As if aware that her aunt didn't want her to wake, the baby opened her green eyes, her tiny face creasing into tearful lines.

'It's all right, darling,' Templar crooned softly, glaring resentfully at the door as the knocking resumed and the petulant voice of her landlady shouted through the rickety door.

'I know you're in there, Miss Newman!' A harsh laugh accompanied this statement. 'Where else would you be?' she mumbled to herself, but loud enough for Templar to hear and be angered by it.

Templar opened the door angrily, standing in the doorway and effectively stopping the other woman entering as she attempted to walk in uninvited. A woman in her fifties, Mrs Marks was nothing if not curious. Templar was far too polite to call her nosy, but in truth that was actually what she was. Templar had had to put up with her unmistakable innuendoes about Keri's parentage when she had first moved in, and she had never forgotten those hurtful remarks. The fact that she wasn't really an unmarried mother had nothing to do with this woman, and Templar had chosen not to tell her that she was in fact the baby's aunt and not her mother as everyone assumed.

If she could have found somewhere else as cheap and as convenient for her job she would have moved out long ago. But it was impossible. No one was willing to accept the unnecessary bother of a young baby in their house when they could get just as much money from a single person or a young couple. In fact Templar was surprised that Mrs Marks put up with the occasional noise Keri made with her crying. She had been told about it a couple of times, but how on earth was she supposed to quieten a young baby who was teething, and quite painfully too.

'Yes, Mrs Marks?' she asked stiffly.

'Now don't take that high and mighty tone with me, young lady,' snapped the elderly lady, her breathing laboured from walking up the three long flights of stairs. 'And you no better than you ought to be,' she grumbled.

Templar held herself proudly erect, refusing to show that she was in any way affected by this woman's barbs. 'My morals have nothing to do with you, Mrs Marks,' she replied coolly. 'Now did you want something special, or is this just a social call?' Templar hated letting this woman know she was getting under her skin, but she had had a hard day at work today, and then it had taken her over an hour to get Keri to sleep, and she hardly felt in the mood for pleasantries.

'There's no need to get cheeky with me, young lady. I came up here to tell you that Bert and me have been receiving complaints again. It isn't good enough,' she added for good measure.

Templar sighed heavily, running a harassed hand through her silky hair. 'I'm sorry about the noise, Mrs Marks, but Keri's teething, and I——'

The landlady shook her head. 'I've heard all your excuses before, and it makes no difference. That child does nothing but cry, and when it comes to receiving complaints from my other tenants, then I'm afraid I have to do something about it.'

Templar gasped indignantly. 'Keri does *not* cry all

the time, she's a very placid baby. Goodness, you'd cry
if you were in pain!'

'Well, that's as maybe,' the woman shifted uncomfortably. 'But I'm going to have to ask you to leave.'

'To—to *leave*—?' Templar trailed off. 'But I—I
have nowhere else to go!'

The other woman's face softened slightly. 'I'm sorry,
love,' she said more gently. 'If it was left to me I'd
probably let you stay, but my Bert's adamant about it.
He wants your room vacated by the end of the week.'

'But—' Templar's face was pale, her movements
slow, 'where can I go?'

'Well, I'm sure I don't know,' Mrs Marks replied
shortly. 'Can't that young man of yours help you out?'

She shook her head dazedly. She couldn't ask Ken
for help. He thought she was behaving stupidly anyway, insisting that she put Keri in a home and marry
him. Until he had said that she had seriously been considering him as a prospective husband, but how could
she marry a man who rejected a defenceless baby? The
idea was unthinkable, and even if things did become so
desperate that she did have to part with Keri, she
certainly wouldn't marry Ken. 'No, I——' she broke
off as Keri began crying, a loud choking sob that pierced
the paper-thin walls.

Mrs Marks frowned deeply. 'You see,' she said with
satisfaction. 'Not a moment's peace. Oh, I feel sorry for
the poor little mite, but I'd feel even more sorry for her
if I didn't have to listen to that noise all night.' She
turned away from the door. 'Remember, the end of the
week.'

How could she forget! Unthinkingly Templar
picked up Keri, cradling her against the thinness of her
own body. As if she realised something was very wrong
with her aunt, Keri's sobs ceased instantly and she

cuddled into Templar's warm scented neck, blowing bubbles and chattering tiredly in the baby talk that endeared her to everyone she met. Or at least, *almost* everyone, Templar thought hardly.

For the next two days Templar spent all of her lunch-hour and part of the evenings searching for new accommodation. But it was hopeless. The ones she could afford wouldn't accept Keri, and the ones she couldn't afford didn't seem to mind the presence of a young baby. It was all so frustrating, and Ken didn't help either.

'Put the kid in an orphanage and marry me,' was all the help he could give her, as Templar had known it would be.

She held on to her temper with difficulty. 'I refuse point blank to part with Keri, she's all the family I have left.'

Ken sighed. 'We could have a family of our own, once we'd settled down, of course.'

'If you feel that way, why couldn't we keep Keri as well?' To keep Keri with her Templar would go to any lengths, even marry this man she didn't love.

'I don't want someone else's child,' Ken said coldly, looking with dislike at Keri as she played happily on the floor.

She didn't bother to answer him. He was at least someone to talk to, a friend, something she was much in need of at the moment. It was surprising how many of the people she had thought were friends had shunned her when they thought Keri was her baby. Only Ken and Mary had remained loyal, Ken because he hoped eventually to wear her down enough to marry him, and Mary because she was a true friend.

She bent and picked Keri up in her arms. 'Come on, poppet. Time for your bath.'

'Couldn't that wait until later?' complained Ken. 'I don't see much of you as it is.'

'Babies need routine.'

'So you keep saying, but when do you have time to take care of yourself?'

She laughed lightly. 'Is that a polite way of saying I look awful? Really, Ken, you aren't very complimentary!' Her green eyes twinkled at him teasingly.

Ken flushed uncomfortably. 'You know very well I didn't mean anything of the sort. You always look beautiful, and you know it.'

Templar knew she was attractive, as an ex-model she would be stupid not to know that. It wasn't conceited to know that her long auburn hair shone like autumn leaves, that her wide uptilted eyes, small nose, and wide generous mouth made up a beautiful face, and that her body was perfectly proportioned, if slightly thinner now than it should be. But most of all it was her complete naturalness that finished her beauty, giving her an inner glow that many beautiful women throughout the world paid much money for and never attained.

At the moment her hair was tied back from her face, showing clearly her high cheekbones and slender swan-like neck. Up until a year ago she had been a model, but the unusual times, the long hours of work, and the travelling, as well as caring for Keri, had made it impossible for her to carry on. She had been forced to fall back on the secretarial qualifications she had obtained when she was at school, accepting a job that had little prospects and paid much less money than she had been earning. And she hadn't been a model long enough for her to have saved much money, and what there had been was slowly wasting away. Almost every week she withdrew a small amount of her savings, and each week the amount seemed to be larger than the last.

Luckily Templar knew how to care for her hair expertly so that the loss of visits to the hair salon had made no difference to her long straight tresses, and her skin was smooth enough not to require any cosmetics whatsoever. Occasionally she applied mascara and a light lipstick, but as the money became more and more scarce, these occasions became almost never.

'Do you want to help me bath her?' she asked as she gathered the baby's nightclothes together.

'No, thanks.' Ken picked up the newspaper, burying his nose in its depths.

She didn't attempt to argue with him, well aware that Keri welcomed his company no more than he did hers. With the perception of the very young, Keri soon learnt who liked her and who didn't.

This was the time of day Templar enjoyed the most, with Keri splashing about in the water with her toys, and usually wetting the bathroom more than she did herself. Templar looked down at the copper curls with love. It was strange really how Keri had inherited none of Tiffany's blonde-haired, blue-eyed beauty, but all of her aunt's colouring and sense of fun.

She looked up now and dimpled at her aunt. 'M— Ma—Ma——' she gurgled happily.

'Mama, Mama,' encouraged Templar. 'Come on, darling, say it. Mama, Mama.'

'Ma—Ma,' her little tongue wrestled with the word, still not quite managing to say the word properly and losing interest as she began gurgling again.

'You're a monkey,' Templar laughed. 'A monkey,' she repeated as the little girl looked up interestedly.

Keri was rosy-cheeked and fresh-smelling when they re-entered the room, her tiny fingers clutching on to Templar's hair. She kissed the baby gently on the cheek before laying her down in her cot. 'Now off to sleep with you,' she grinned down at the baby. 'Keri be a good girl.'

'That'd make a change,' mumbled Ken, emerging from behind the newspaper.

'She's a very good baby,' Templar returned calmly. 'You don't like children, that's all.'

'Oh, but I do. At least, I'll like my own. I just resent the fact that Keri has no real claim on you. You just took over the responsibility of her after your sister died. I said you were stupid then, and I think you're even more so now. That child is draining you physically as well as financially. You could have been one of the best paid models in the world by now, but instead you——'

'Chose to give Keri all the love she needs rather than fob her off with a nanny or put her into a home,' she cut in. 'We've had this argument many times before, and it gets us nowhere. I love Keri, and I intend keeping her.'

'Okay, okay, on your own head be it. What I can't understand is why you don't know who her father is. Surely Tiffany could have told you?'

'She refused to. She didn't want anything from him, she couldn't possibly have known she was going to die and so never need him again.' A sob caught in her throat as she remembered her young sister, so full of life and not a care in the world. Until this unwanted pregnancy. But at least Tiffany had loved Keri's father, of that she was certain. But as far as she knew he hadn't wanted Tiffany once he found out about the baby. And so at the great age of nineteen her sister had departed this world with hardly a ripple, and her errant boyfriend hadn't so much as made one enquiry about her.

'Keri is *my* child,' she insisted. 'At least, in every way it's possible for her to be without my actually bear-

ing her. I could no more give her up than I could—
than I could stop living!'

Templar took Keri with her to visit Mary the next
day. It was her half day and she usually tried to see her
friend on these occasions. She could have better spent
this time searching for somewhere new to live, but she
made it a habit to always spend this time with Keri.
Goodness knows she spent little enough time with her
as it was.

Mary was, as usual, pleased to see her. With two
little girls and a third baby on the way and only a two-
bedroomed flat, Mary and her husband were in just as
much difficulty as Templar was. It gave them a mutual
grievance. Although there wasn't much difference in
their ages, Mary was worn down with the weight of her
family problems, and Templar dreaded getting into the
same predicament.

'Hello, poppet,' Mary tickled Keri under the chin.
'My, she's getting bonny!' She looked closely at her
friend. 'But you don't look too good. What's happened?'
she asked perceptively.

Templar explained about Mrs Marks' ultimatum
and her difficulty in finding somewhere else to live.

'Oh, dear,' sighed Mary worriedly. 'You could always come here for a few days if you get really stuck
for a place,' she offered.

Templar knew this was a generous act on the part of
her friend, but not one she could possibly accept. 'No,
I'll work something out, thank you, Mary. You can
guess what Ken suggested,' she added dryly.

'Oh, Ken!' Mary dismissed him in disgust. 'He's no
help at all.'

Templar laughed. 'Never mind that for now. I've
brought some apples, so we can make a pie for tea. You
make the pastry and I'll prepare the apples. Deal?'

'Deal. Leave Keri with Samantha, they can play together.'

It was nice to forget their troubles for a little while, laughing like two schoolgirls as they both got flour in their hair. 'We're worse than the children,' giggled Templar as she tried to get the flour out of her hair and off the tip of her nose.

'You aren't much more than a child yourself,' teased Mary. 'What are you? Twenty-one, twenty-two?'

'Twenty-one,' she confirmed. 'A year older than Tiffany would have been. I often wonder what it would have been like if she'd lived. I could have worked and supported them both. I could, you know. My career was just expanding nicely. It seems so cruel that she had to die. She hadn't even begun to live, she was just a child.'

'And you've never heard from Keri's father?' put in Mary gently.

Templar shook her head. 'It's as if he never existed,' she laughed bitterly. 'But I have her to prove that he did. I think he must be rather a handsome man if Keri's looks are anything to go by. Oh, I know she has my colouring, but her features are nothing like mine, or Tiffany's for that matter. And her complexion is much darker than either of us.'

'Did you ever look through those letters of Tiffany's? You know, the ones in that carved box.'

She shook her head. 'No, I couldn't. It would be like violating Tiffany's privacy. Those letters were addressed to her, and it would be wrong of me to read them.'

'But you don't actually have to read them,' Mary pointed out. 'Just look at the signatures and addresses. Surely you could do that without reading them?'

'I suppose so,' Templar agreed reluctantly. 'But I just don't think I can.'

'Of course you can,' her friend insisted impatiently. 'This isn't the time to worry about a little thing like privacy. Or pride either, for that matter.'

Templar knew she was right. Tiffany had kept a box of letters, but Templar had never been able to force herself to look at them, although she felt sure Keri's father's name would be in there somewhere.

Once she had settled Keri down for the night she took the box out of the cupboard, staring fixedly at it for several minutes before opening its wooden lid. She hesitated for a moment more, unwilling to delve into secrets that were perhaps better left alone.

Taking a deep breath, she began flicking through the letters, only glancing fleetingly at the signature on each and ignoring their other contents. It didn't take all that long to find the one she thought might be helpful. Never a secretive girl, Tiffany had spoken freely about her boy-friends, and so Templar knew most of the names on the letters. Only one was unknown to her, and she could only assume this was Keri's father. It had been unlike Tiffany not to tell her sister everything, that was why it had been all the more surprising that she wouldn't reveal the name of her lover.

Templar put the other letters back in the box, putting off the moment when she would actually have to read the letter. It just didn't seem right to read someone else's personal letters. Finally, she couldn't put it off any longer, slowly reading the slightly faded words. There were faint smudges on the two pages of the letter, as if someone had been crying as they read them, which Templar could well imagine was true after reading their contents. Alex Marcose had said quite plainly that he wouldn't be seeing Tiffany any more. No mention was made of the baby, but the date at the top of the letter fitted in with the time Tiffany must have found out about her pregnancy, so Templar imagined the baby must have been the reason he had broken off the relationship. Well, she was afraid that things like babies had a way of making their presence felt. And Mr Alex Marcose was about to be informed of his daughter's existence.

She posted the letter to the London address the next day, informing Mr Marcose that she had something of import to tell him. But this didn't stop her from searching for accommodation. Mr Marcose might not still live at that address, and even if he did, her name might be enough to put him off. The address was in one of the better parts of town, and people like that had a way of forgetting their responsibilities. He might even have forgotten Tiffany's existence.

It was three days since Templar had posted the letter, and she had received no reply, although she was sure it must have reached its destination by now. And she still hadn't found anywhere to live! The situation was becoming desperate now, and she was hardly sleeping at night, and worrying incessantly by day. And Keri wasn't helping either, being particularly fretful the past few days, sensitive to her aunt's worry.

She went in to her for the third time in an hour, soon quietening her and going back to her magazine. She tried to concentrate on the article she was reading, but the words seemed to make no sense, and putting the magazine down on the floor she curled her legs up underneath her and resting her head back on the chair, she fell asleep.

She was woken up by the knock on the door, pushing back her untidy hair and smoothing down her creased denims. If it was Mrs Marks again, she'd——

The knock sounded again. 'Miss Newman! Miss Newman! I have a visitor for you.'

A visitor! Oh, God! Who on earth could it be? It must be someone Mrs Marks didn't know or she wouldn't have accompanied them up the stairs. Templar glanced apprehensively at the half-closed bedroom door, but couldn't hear any movement from Keri. Thank goodness for that; she didn't think she could stand for her to wake up again.

She opened the door, her eyes opening wide with shock as they encountered the tall alien-looking man standing arrogantly at Mrs Marks' side. Her landlady looked quite overwhelmed, and Templar wasn't surprised. The man was looking down his haughty nose at both of them, his suit fitting him as if it had been tailored on him, and it probably had been.

'You—er——' Templar hesitated. 'You can go now, Mrs Marks,' she said firmly, watching the landlady as she slowly began to descend the stairs, muttering to herself as she went. Templar looked at the man again, only to find herself the victim of a contemptuous perusal, his blue-grey eyes mentally noting each feature as if for future reference. 'Would you like to come in?' she asked nervously.

'You are very trusting, Miss Newman,' his accent was faintly clipped, as if English wasn't his native tongue. 'Considering you do not know who I am.' He held himself erect. 'My name is Leondro Marcose.'

'Oh, but——'

He held up a hand for silence. 'Before you say any more, Miss Newman, I think you should know that my brother Alex is dead.' He said the words with no show of emotion.

Templar paled. This wasn't what she had been expecting at all. How could he cold-heartedly stand there and tell her such a thing! Her only chance of a future for Keri now in ruins. Tears filled her emerald green

eyes and threatened to overspill. She was going to lose
Keri, and there wasn't a thing she could do about it.

This stranger was still staring at her as if he were dis-
secting her, and even in her distress Templar could see
he was devastatingly attractive. And Alex, Keri's father,
had been his brother. If there had been any resemblance between the two brothers then Tiffany couldn't
be blamed for her attraction. Templar still held the
door open for him to enter, and without waiting for her
to repeat the invitation he entered the room, looking
about him without concealing his distaste.

She saw the shabby room through his eyes and her
resentment towards him grew. Who was he to look
down his nose at her when she had been struggling for
the past year to support his brother's daughter?—maybe not in the way he would have done, but one thing
Keri had never gone short of was love. 'I see,' she said
tightly. 'In that case I'm afraid you've had a wasted
journey. You can't possibly help me.'

His eyebrows rose arrogantly at her dismissive tone.
'Please allow me to be the judge of that, Miss Newman.
Your letter sounded urgent, otherwise I would not have
come here at all. You say I cannot help you. What
makes you think my brother could have done more than
I?' His eyes flickered mercilessly over her nervous
movements. 'Will you not sit down, so that I may also?'

'Oh! Oh, I'm sorry.' She sat down in the chair she
had recently vacated.

'So,' he sat opposite her. 'Would you mind telling
me what it was only my brother could help you with?'
His eyes narrowed to two icy slits. 'Or is it so private
you cannot tell me about it?'

Templar's eyes flashed angrily at his condescending
tone. 'You aren't being very polite, Mr Marcose.'

'Am I not?' he asked tautly. 'But then you are being

particularly obstructive. You sent an urgent letter to my brother and when I come in his stead you refuse to tell me what the matter was you wanted to discuss with him.' He stood up in one fluid movement, a ripple of pure ripcord muscle the only sign of effort. 'It seems you are right, and I have had a wasted journey.'

Templar stood up to aid his departure, but was prevented from doing so by an ear-piercing scream from Keri. Without waiting to answer his look of astonishment she dashed into the bedroom, her only thought to quieten her before she disturbed the whole household. Keri raised tear-wet cheeks and Templar couldn't resist her endearing little face. 'There, darling,' she crooned softly. 'It's all right, my baby.'

Leondro Marcose stood transfixed in the doorway, his darkly handsome face a shuttered mask. 'So,' he said harshly, the voice that she had thought attractive grating with suppressed violence. 'You have a child.'

'As you can see.' Templar still smiled reassuringly at Keri.

Keri's big green eyes fixed themselves on the tall dark man's face, and she chuckled delightedly. 'Mama,' she chortled. 'Mama.'

To Templar it was a triumph, but it only seemed to incense her visitor more, if that were possible. Ignoring his censorious look, she smiled happily at Keri. 'Aren't you clever, darling. Now are you going to go back to sleep? Mama has a visitor, and you're being very naughty.'

'Please do not hurry yourself because of me.' The man's voice was like a rapier, cutting all down before him, and at the moment it was her. 'If *this* is the reason you wanted my brother's help, then you are right, I can be of no service to you. You have formed your own destiny, and to involve other people in your troubles is not something I appreciate.'

'Really, Mr Marcose?' she asked tartly, taking Keri over to this tall imperious stranger and placing her in front of him. He had little choice but to take the squirming bundle into his strong arms, staring at her intently.

Templar waited with bated breath as Keri played with the buttons on the front of his snowy white shirt, her four tiny white teeth showing between ruby-red lips. Leondro Marcose looked from Keri to Templar and back again, his face pale.

'This child,' his voice was husky and curiously uncertain. 'There is no doubt that you are the child's mother. And the father——' he stopped. 'The father was my brother, was he not?'

She nodded. 'Yes, he was. But I——'

'Please!' he said curtly, carrying Keri into the other room where he sat down abruptly in one of the armchairs. Keri looked at him with gleeful eyes, enjoying this unexpected treat. Men didn't very often come into her orbit, except Ken of course, and as their dislike was mutual he didn't count. As Leondro Marcose looked at her his face softened, the harsh lines beside his firm mouth dissipating. 'And what is your name, little one?'

'Her name is Keri,' put in Templar. 'And she's ten months old.' She still hadn't told him that Keri wasn't her child, but somehow now didn't seem to be the right moment.

'I see.' He looked at her over Keri's copper curls. 'And of what assistance can I be to you?'

She looked taken aback. 'Why, none,' she said in a surprised voice. 'It was your brother I wanted to see, and as he's—dead,' the word choked in her throat. Poor Keri, both parents dead so young. 'As he's dead,

I'll have to solve my problem on my own.'

'I disagree. Must I remind you that Keri is my niece?'

Templar was dumbstruck. It was an aspect she hadn't thought of. She shook her head. 'You only have my word for that. I couldn't swear Alex was her father.'

'The devil you can't!' he rasped, and Keri's face puckered tearfully at the harshness of his voice. 'It is all right, little one.' He placed her on the floor and stood up to pace the room, taking out a long cigar and a gold lighter. 'I have your permission to smoke?' he asked grimly, igniting the lighter at the nod of her head. He didn't speak again for several long seconds. 'So you do not know if my brother is your baby's father, or if she belongs to one of your other lovers,' he addressed her coolly. 'Well, let me put your mind at rest. Keri is Alexis' child, of that there can be no doubt. She is very like him to look at. Have you not noticed the resemblance? Or have you forgotten how my brother looked in the sea of faces that were no doubt your lovers?'

Templar blanched under his insults. 'And what do you intend doing, Mr Marcose? Paying me off?'

His mouth twisted tauntingly. 'That is the one thing I do not intend doing, Miss Newman. I'm sure that you expected as much from Alex, but you will find I am made of much sterner stuff than my brother was. No, Keri is my niece and I intend taking her into my care. If I gave you money you would no doubt spend it on things other than the infant, and although I realise you have a certain amount of affection for the child, I am sure you will appreciate that I can give her more than you will ever be able to. No matter how many men you take into your bed.'

She hit out at him instinctively, her only thought to hurt him as he was verbally hurting her. Her finger marks stood out livid against his dark skin and she moved away from him in horror, snatching the frightened Keri off the floor and hugging her tightly against her. The two of them looked at him with apprehensive eyes, Templar noting a strange expression cross his face, but it passed so fleetingly she didn't have time to analyse it. 'I do not have a "certain amount of affection" for Keri,' she said in a low controlled voice. 'I love her. And no—no *stranger* is going to take her away from me. Oh, I know you can give her more than I can, you're obviously wealthy enough to, but I *love* her. Doesn't that mean anything to you?'

'Not a great deal,' he replied coldly. 'And as you know I have money I do not think there was any need for that remark about my being wealthy. Alexis must have told you it was so and you obviously thought it was time to play your lead card. As a small baby Keri may not have made the impact that she has now, especially as she has your hair and eyes. But then most babies look alike. But now, now that her features are becoming distinctly like my brother's you decide the time is right to make us aware of her existence. What is the matter, Miss Newman? Are you tired of caring for a young baby? Do you long to go back to the life you no doubt led before my young brother was gullible enough to fall for your undoubted charms?'

She shook her head. This just couldn't be happening to her! Oh, she realised the remark she had made about being unsure of Keri's parentage had sparked off this cold chilling anger, but if he had only given her chance she could have explained that her uncertainty was due to the fact that Keri was not her child. Now it had gone too far. If she told him the truth now he would probably take Keri away from her altogether, and then she might never see her again. 'Keri is my life now,' she said simply. 'And I won't let you take her from me.'

'You would not be able to stop me if that were my intention. If none of your—admirers would be willing to come forward I am sure I could find a couple of men who would give evidence against you. I only have to cast doubts on your ability to be a proper mother and Keri will be given into my care. Do you want that?'

'You think money can buy everything, don't you, Mr Marcose?' she said brokenly.

'Please, call me Leon, anything else would be verging on the ridiculous in the circumstances. And I shall call you——?' he paused expectantly.

'Templar,' she replied miserably.

'Unusual,' came his comment. 'And no, I know money cannot buy everything. Most things, but not everything. But in this case it will get me what I want.'

'And what is that?' Templar asked dully, cradling the now sleepy Keri against her.

'I wish to make a future for Keri. I cannot do that by taking her into my house as my brother's child. Everyone will know her for what she is, and that I do not want. She is a beautiful child and deserves to have the sort of background I would wish for her. So I propose to marry her mother and so pass Keri off as my own child.'

CHAPTER TWO

'WHAT!' Templar stared at him in horror. 'You can't possibly be serious?'

Arrogant eyebrows rose over heavy-lidded eyes, the firmness of his mouth showing his displeasure. 'But I am, perfectly serious. The final decision does of course lie with you. You can either give up your daughter or marry me.'

Templar placed Keri back in her cot, moving like an automaton. She wrung her hands together, her eyes dwelling thoughtfully on the copper curls just visible from the bedroom. She looked again at the dark forbidding face of the man who had the power to wreck her whole life, and saw no softening there, he obviously meant what he said.

His thick dark hair was brushed casually back from his high forehead, his nostrils flaring arrogantly as she continued to look at him. How could she let her little Keri live with this hard, embittered man, with no one to give her a mother's love? Or would he get someone else to provide that? He was a very determined man and a little thing like *her* unhappiness wouldn't matter to him as long as he got what he wanted. And there could be no doubt that he wanted Keri. If she told him now that Keri wasn't her child he would take her away from her anyway; much better to keep that knowledge to herself. As long as this man attained control of his niece what possible difference could it make that Templar wasn't her mother? As far as she could see it would only be Keri and herself who suffered by his gaining such information.

'Why—' her lips felt stiff and she found it difficult to articulate. 'Why should you want to do a thing like that?' she asked nervously, licking her lips.

His expression didn't alter as he flicked a speck off the tailored jacket of his light grey suit. 'Why should I not?' he returned coolly. 'And do not obtain the mistaken idea that I am considering this course of action for any other reason than Keri's future. You, as a person, do not interest me in the slightest. Secondhand goods are not my line.'

'And just what *is* your line, Mr Marcose?' she asked, ignoring his insults as she felt sure he wanted to annoy her, and she wouldn't give him that satisfaction.

'Surely Alex told you?'

He sounded slightly mocking and Templar flushed uncomfortably. 'No,' she answered lightly. 'I don't believe your occupation ever entered into our conversation, in fact, I don't think we ever discussed you at all.' Which happened to be true. How could she have discussed anything with a man she had never met?

His eyes darkened to a metallic grey. 'Alex seems to have been remiss concerning several of his relationships. I had never heard of you either. Just what was your line before you had Keri?'

Templar bridled angrily at his condescending tone. 'My line, as you put it, happened to be modelling.'

'Really? Alex seems to have found girls in that profession particularly attractive for some reason.' His eyes studied her intently. 'Ah, yes, I remember now. When I first saw you I thought you appeared familiar. You are the girl in the make-up advertisement, are you not?'

Her nose wrinkled slightly at his obvious distaste. 'That was one of my last assignments,' she remembered wistfully.

'You would like to return to your profession?'

Templar shook her head. 'Not now. It's too late. I have Keri and she's my whole life.'

Her visitor looked bored. 'You do not have to continually try to convince me of your devotion to the child. I have given you the options, you have only to make your choice.'

She paced restlessly about the room. 'It's not as simple as that,' she insisted.

'I see. You have a—boy-friend?'

Momentarily Templar thought of Ken and then dismissed him. He could hardly be cast in the light Leondro Marcose was trying to put him in. 'No, I have no boy-friend.'

'You surprise me,' he said dryly.

'I have a male friend, but that's *all* he is,' she said firmly. 'Anyway, that isn't the reason for my hesitation. You can't honestly expect me to seriously consider marriage to a man I've known barely an hour, a man that I know nothing about. You claim to be Keri's uncle, but I only have your word for that.'

'Do not be hysterical!' he snapped. 'If it is information about myself that you want then I will gladly tell you a few facts about myself. My name you already know. I am thirty-six years of age, and unmarried. I have worldwide business interests, mainly hotels and property. I am Greek, but I live mainly in my apartment in London. Of course, if you decide to marry me, I will move you into my house in the country. I shall be taking Keri there anyway, whatever you decide to do. A nanny will be obtained for her.'

'It most certainly will not!' Templar said adamantly. 'If, and I emphasise the if, I allow you to force me into this senseless marriage, I will continue to care for Keri myself. Goodness, I could have arranged for a nanny for her myself and carried on working to pay for her.

But I don't think that's the way to bring up a child. It would be heartless to do that to her now, she has come to rely on me completely.'

He gave a slight inclination of his head. 'That is, of course, unfortunate. It seems you have little choice in the matter, then.' He stood up.

She stayed his departure, her face desperate. 'Please! Look, couldn't you just care for Keri and myself? We could—well, we could still come and live with you. But surely *we* don't have to marry?'

'The idea appeals to me no more than it does you. But Keri's likeness to Alex is too noticeable for her to be other than his child—or my own. And in this case I would prefer that she was thought to be mine. Alex may have had a fleeting relationship with you, but in Greece he has a fiancée who could be hurt by your mere existence. In your country it may be accepted that women have children outside of marriage, but such a thing would not be allowed to happen in my country.'

'Must I remind you that it was your brother who was responsible for Keri's birth? The woman is not solely to blame for the situation she finds herself in.'

His mouth set in firm lines. 'I realise this. That is why it is only right that I should care for you and your child. It is unfortunate that this has occurred at all, but now that it has, and Alex is no longer alive to face up to his responsibilities, I will have to do so for him.'

'And you think love didn't enter into it?'

His eyes flickered over her contemptuously. 'You are surely not trying to tell me that you *loved* my brother?'

Templar flinched from the derision in his voice. Whatever he thought, Tiffany *had* loved his brother, and there was no denying this fact. 'Surely the fact that Keri was born at all is proof enough. No single woman would bring a child into the world if she didn't love its father—or at least, she doesn't *have* to. It isn't necessary nowadays.'

'Maybe not in your estimation, but in mine every child conceived with love or without it should be given the chance of life. So what you are saying is that if you hadn't loved Alex, Keri would not have been born? And yet a few moments ago you said you were not even sure Alex was her father. Have you been in love with all the men who have shared your bed?' he scorned.

'Mr Marcose,' she began tightly, 'if you have such a bad opinion of me, aren't you taking rather a risk by marrying me? After all, I might be a very disruptive influence in your life.'

'You will not be allowed to be,' he said arrogantly. 'You will lead a very quiet life at my country house.'

'Oh, yes? And just what will you be doing while I keep out of trouble in the country?'

'Working. At my London apartment. I rarely visit the house you would be living in, and as soon as you move there I will endeavour to make my visits even more infrequent. I have no wish to behave as the doting husband too often.'

'The—the *what*?'

He looked impatient. 'We will have to show a certain amount of affection towards one another, no matter how much we hate it. It will be expected.'

Templar shook her head. 'Not by me it won't! I couldn't possibly pretend to feel affection for someone I——' she broke off.

'Hate?' Leondro Marcose suggested. 'You can be assured, Templar Newman, that the feeling is mutual. But I think my brother must have had some feelings of love for you. I do not know if he was aware of the type of person you actually are. Not even to know the father of your own child!' his top lip curled back in a sneer.

'I will leave you now. But arrangements will be made for our marriage of which you will be notified.'

'Couldn't I just have a little time to think it all over?' begged Templar. 'It's all so—so sudden.'

'Why sudden?' he asked tartly. 'You must have expected something of the sort when you wrote that letter.'

She shook her head numbly. 'I didn't. I just thought your brother—Alex,' she amended quickly, 'I thought he might be able to help me.'

'And why is it that you suddenly need this help? Keri is ten months old, did you not consider asking for his assistance when she was born? Ah, but I forgot—you did not know Alex *was* her father. So why this sudden necessity for his aid?'

Templar thought of refusing to answer him, but knew he would only force it out of her. 'I've been told I have to leave here at the end of the week, and I simply have nowhere else to go. No one wants to take in an unmarried mother, and I thought Alex might just be able to help for a couple of months until I had something sorted out.'

'And now you find yourself placed in the position where you either marry someone you hate, or lose the one thing you love. It is a pity, of course, but then you were instrumental in forging your own destiny. You must have known you could never have married Alex.'

'And why should I have known that?'

'Because of his fiancée. A betrothal is almost as binding as a marriage in my country, and Alex was very much betrothed. He was killed only four weeks before the wedding was to have taken place. And do not think you were the first girl he had been involved with. There was another model just before his involvement with you.'

'Then he couldn't have been very much in love with his fiancée, to have behaved that way.'

'Love!' he scoffed. 'What does love have to do with marriage? His betrothed was a quiet girl of a good family and breeding, and she would have brought a large dowry to her husband.'

'Everything I'm not, apparently,' said Templar dryly.

'As you say,' he agreed coldly. 'But obviously your other attributes meant more to him at the time than anything Katina could give him.' He glanced impatiently at his wrist watch. 'I have an important appointment to go to now; you have until Friday to make up your mind. But be assured that whatever you decide to do for yourself, Keri will come to me. You are perfectly free to live your own life.'

'Keri *is* my life,' she repeated vehemently.

'So you have said. I will call again on Friday.'

The room felt strangely empty once he had left, the smell of his cigar lingering in the air. Templar stared blankly at the closed door. Things had seemed desperate before, but they were even worse now. Leondro Marcose might be able to give Keri the sort of upbringing Templar could only dream about for her, but it meant a lifelong marriage for Templar to a man she could only ever despise.

She stood at the side of Keri's cot, tears streaming down her cheeks. 'Oh, darling,' she breathed softly, 'what shall I do? Oh, what shall I do?'

Templar looked around the shabby room she had moved into the day before. When the kindly landlady had told her that she could have the room *and* that she would look after Keri while Templar worked she couldn't believe her luck. She had told no one she was moving, except of course Mrs Marks. Not even Mary and Ken knew. She daren't risk being traced by them. Men like Leondro Marcose could wield a lot of power, and it wouldn't take him long to trace one very frightened girl and her baby.

And she *was* frightened, terrified in fact. She couldn't possibly spend the rest of her life married to that cold arrogant man. He had the look of a springing leopard about to leap on its prey. And Templar felt as if she was that prey.

Keri seemed little bothered by her change of scene, not that it was all that different. All these rooms were the same, although this one was shabbier than most. But then the landlady was kind, and that made all the difference.

Of Ken she had seen little; he had finally washed his hands of her. In fact, like Leondro Marcose, Ken had given her an ultimatum: marry him and give up Keri or else their relationship ended. He seemed to think he had waited long enough for her, and the argument that had followed had not been pleasant. Templar had told him so many times that she would never give up Keri that she had thought he would actually have realised by now that she meant what she said. But he hadn't, accusing her of playing at mother, and Keri's contented gurgles of 'Mama' had only incensed him more. Finally he had stormed out of the room with a vow to waste no more time on her.

In a way his departure had been a relief. His complaints about Keri had become more pronounced of late and Templar often had to bite her tongue from preventing herself from saying something she would regret. Like most red-haired people, she had a hot temper, although she usually managed to control it. As a child she had often been punished for losing her temper with another child, or even more disastrous, with an adult.

At every movement or knock on the door Templar physically jumped, dreading opening the door in case it should be Leondro Marcose, although Keri didn't seem affected by the air of electricity that surrounded her.

Templar took Keri downstairs and left her with Mrs Street. She had to leave earlier in the mornings now, the journey to work taking twice as long from here. Her employer, Howard Hathaway, ran a small insurance agency, and Templar, besides being his secretary, was his assistant, the tea-girl, general telephonist and also the cleaning lady. Not that she minded. A huge impersonal complex wasn't her idea of enjoying work, although occasionally Howard became just a little too familiar. Templar never ceased to be amazed by this. Howard had a beautiful and loving wife and two young children, and yet still he had to try and prove his irresistible manhood—another reason for her disillusionment of men's fidelity.

'Good morning, Howard,' she said breathlessly, placing her bag full of groceries in the corner of the room with her coat. 'Sorry I'm late, but I just had to get some food in.'

'That's all right,' accepted Howard, a man in his mid-thirties beginning to go slightly bald on top. 'Although you look worn out before you even start. What have you been up to?'

'Why, nothing,' she blushed. 'But Keri did have rather a wakeful night last night.'

'Teething,' sympathised Howard. Having had to put up with it twice himself he knew how wearing it could be.

Templar shook her head, beginning to sort through

the letters on her desk. 'No, it wasn't teething. She decided that two o'clock this morning was the time to play,' she grimaced. 'You try telling a determined ten-month-old that you're too tired to play! It doesn't work.'

'I know,' he laughed. 'Look, leave those for a minute and make us both a cup of coffee.'

Templar went round to see Mary at lunch-time. She didn't think she would be able to bring Keri over so often now that they were living further away, although there was a park near them now so she would be able to take her there. Fresh air was something neither of them had enough of.

'Hello, love,' Mary greeted her in surprise. 'What brings you round? Not that it isn't nice to see you, but you don't usually call on a Friday.'

'Well, I—' Templar hesitated about revealing her change of address, not that she didn't trust Mary, but from what she had seen of Leondro Marcose she thought he could be completely ruthless on occasion. And it wasn't fair to involve Mary in her troubles, she had enough of her own. She smiled brightly at her friend. 'I just felt like coming round. It's a lovely day outside, why don't we go out for a walk? We could do some window-shopping.'

'Mm, lovely. Just wait a minute while I get my coat. Samantha's at nursery school this morning,' Mary sighed. 'At least by the time this one's born she'll be old enough to join Melanie at school. Peter will insist on trying for a boy,' she smiled slightly. 'Men and their male ego!'

Templar couldn't have agreed more, although she didn't say so. It was relaxing to walk around the shops, even if neither of them could afford to buy anything. Occasionally Templar would see one of her old crowd when out on these walks, but besides a polite hello she didn't attempt any conversation with them.

Howard was in one of his more boisterous moods when she got back to the office and she could only assume he had been on one of his selling lunches again. When this happened he *and* the client had usually drunk so much that neither of them could remember what policies had or had not been taken out. Without saying a word Templar prepared him some black coffee, placing it unquestionably before him.

'What's this for?' He looked at her through bleary eyes.

'Drink it, Howard,' she said quietly. 'It will do you good.'

'Are you implying I'm drunk?' he asked sneeringly.

Templar didn't know what to say; as usual the drink had made Howard nasty and the best thing for her to do was keep out of his way. She moved quietly away from him and didn't see his quick movement as he put out a hand and pulled her down on to his knees.

'Howard!' She was deeply shocked. No matter how much he had drunk he wasn't usually like this. 'Stop it!'

'What's the matter, girl?' he snapped. 'You weren't always so fussy, were you? What about that little bast——'

'Don't you dare say that, Howard! Don't you dare! Keri was born out of love, not what you're implying.' She struggled to get out of his arms. 'I think you've said quite enough for one day!'

'I could not agree more.'

Templar stopped struggling at the sound of that cold clipped voice and looked up, straight into the contemptuous blue-grey eyes of Leondro Marcose. He was looking at the two of them as if they were something rather nasty that had wandered into his line of vision. She stood up, smoothing down her plain navy-coloured skirt and straightening her pure white blouse.

Howard struggled to his feet, shifting uncomfortably under the other man's cold stare. 'Who the hell are you?' he blustered.

Leondro Marcose moved further into the tiny office that Howard rented, looking scathingly at the untidy clutter that was their work. 'I am Leondro Marcose. But I might ask you the same question? Also, what you were doing to my fiancée when I entered the office?'

Howard looked at Templar with dazed eyes, and well he might; she was a little dazed herself. 'Your fian——? Leondro Marcose——? You didn't tell me you were engaged,' he added accusingly.

Leondro Marcose looked down his haughty nose at the red-faced man. 'I was not aware that Templar had to inform you of happenings in her personal life—except of course in connection with tendering her notice,' he flicked an imaginary speck off his suit jacket.

Templar glanced at him sharply, her gratitude at his intervention now turning to suspicion. What was he doing here anyway? She didn't remember telling him where she worked, unless of course Mrs Marks had——? But no, surely not. But then what did it really matter how he had found her, he had, and she had a feeling that he would wait no longer for her decision—or at least, no longer than it took him to get her out of here. Not that she wanted to stay under the circumstances. Howard had been very insulting, the remarks he made about Keri unforgivable, and his behaviour had been too familiar for her to carry on working for him any longer.

'What notice?' Howard demanded. 'I haven't been told about any notice being given.'

'It was to have been tendered today, Mr Hathaway,' the tall alien-looking man informed him coldly. 'But your behaviour has made that unnecessary. In the circumstances I am sure you will realise that I can do no other than remove Templar from your unwanted attentions,' he turned to Templar. 'Are you ready to leave now?'

She moved jerkily, collecting her coat and shopping before following her 'fiancé' as he moved back towards the door. Surprisingly Howard detained her just as she was leaving, clutching frantically at her arm.

'Templar! Please,' he begged as she turned to look at him with cool green eyes. 'I'm sorry, Templar, I really am.' The arrogance of Leondro Marcose had sobered him more quickly than any coffee would have done.

She removed his hand from her arm. 'It was the drink talking, Howard, I realise that. But you must realise I can't possibly stay here any longer, not knowing the way you feel about Keri and myself.' She was ever conscious of Leondro Marcose's chilling features and wondered how she could ever leave with him.

Howard stepped back away from her as he saw the frosty looks he was receiving from the man at her side. He had been taken slightly off guard when this man had walked in, but now he wondered how Templar could possibly have met such an imposing man. This man's reputation as a ruthless businessman was known worldwide, and Howard would hardly have put Templar in the society he was likely to mix in. But then Templar had been an up-and-coming model before she had her baby, so perhaps this was the child's father. It wouldn't surprise him. He was a handsome devil in an aristocratic sort of way and there was no doubting Templar's beauty, enough to catch the eye of any man.

Leondro Marcose's eyes narrowed at the dawning realisation in Howard's face. 'If you will excuse us,' he nodded stiffly, opening the door that Templar had little choice but to go through. He gave her chance to say nothing until he had her firmly seated in the luxurious sports car he had parked outside. 'Now you may talk,' he said haughtily, his face intent on the traffic as he manoeuvred the car along the busy streets.

'I have nothing to say.' She held herself erect, unwilling to relax back in the comfortable seat. She felt as if she were riding on a cloud, and by the sleek line of the car she guessed it was a foreign make. Not that she knew much about cars, she couldn't tell the brake from the accelerator.

He looked at her with amusement. 'If what you say is true then you are truly a remarkable woman. You are the first one I have found to be so silent.'

'Then you can't have met many women,' she replied tartly. 'I know many women who like to sit quietly.'

'Ah, now that is different. I too know many women who like to sit quietly, but that does not mean that you cannot see they have plenty they would like to say. As to my not knowing many women, I can assure you that I have not lived for thirty-six years without coming to know the complexities of women very well. I, like you, have had many—acquaintances, shall we say?'

'I understand, Mr Marcose. I understand perfectly!'

'No, you do not. But it is unimportant that you do,' he glanced sideways at her. 'And my name is Leon—use it.'

She bit her lips to stop them trembling. All her efforts to never see this man again had been futile. She should have realised that a man of his arrogance and bearing would not let an insignificant nonentity like herself stop him from getting what he wanted. Well, perhaps she wasn't completely insignificant, she was Keri's mother after all.

'I can't call you Leon,' she said finally when she had her emotions under better control. 'You may be Keri's uncle, but that doesn't give you any special privileges where I'm concerned. If you're anything like her father then I would rather not have met you at all. My meeting with Alex was born out of necessity rather than choice.'

'And does the fact that he is dead and unable to help you make your need any less important?' he snapped harshly. 'Or are you willing to carry on as you have been doing, barely managing to support the two of you and having to accept your employer's pawing in an effort to hold on to your job?'

There could be no doubt about it, Leondro Marcose was furiously angry. Up until now Templar had seen him condescending, arrogant, chillingly cool, and just downright rude, but never angry. In anger his eyes became a steely grey and his face gained an animation she found fascinating. But no, this man was made out of the same mould as his brother, taking his pleasures where he could and leaving the woman involved without a second thought, if indeed he had had first ones.

'I would welcome your pawing even less,' she told him vehemently.

'You will never be given the opportunity to welcome or reject my touch.' His eyes flickered over her insolently, from the auburn glory of her hair, over her make-upless face, and slowly down over her naturally slender body. She heaved a sigh of relief when the traffic lights changed to green, his attention once again centred on the road. 'You do not attract me in the slightest,' he added cruelly.

'You can be assured that the feeling is reciprocated!'

'Good,' he said with some satisfaction. 'And now that we have disposed of that little matter perhaps we can attempt an unemotional conversation. I would like to know what you think you have achieved by changing your address?'

'Nothing, obviously.'

'You hoped to evade making a decision one way or the other?' Leondro Marcose queried mildly. 'But surely you did not think that once I knew of Keri's existence I would calmly leave you to make your choice? But no! You have a noticeably stubborn streak in your nature, Templar Newman, and I guessed you might attempt something of this nature. You have been closely watched since we last spoke together.'

'I've been *what*?'

'You have been watched,' he repeated calmly.

She looked at him sharply. 'So you've been checking up on me? And how many men were reported to have visited my flat?' she asked sneeringly.

'Only one. And apparently he did not look too pleased when he left the premises.'

'Really? Oh dear, I must be slipping. My men usually go away satisfied,' she told him shrilly.

'Templar!' he snapped, looking at her darkly. 'You will not talk in this way.'

'Why not? It's what you expect of me, isn't it, that men come to see me for one reason only?' Her green eyes flashed her anger.

'I have not said so,' he replied stiffly.

'No, but you've implied it.'

He shook his dark head. 'Not in the way that you are saying it. If I thought that you went to bed with every man you met then Keri's future would already have been settled—I would simply have taken her away from you. No, I believe that you have a certain amount of affection for the men you—please, otherwise you would not still have Keri in your care. I would have removed her straight away.'

'Well, thank you very much for your faith in my morals, *Mr Marcose*, but I don't need it. What you do or do not think doesn't make any difference to me. I wouldn't marry you if you were the last man on earth!'

'Not even for the baby?' he asked softly.

'Not even for her!'

With a tightening of his mouth he made no comment and Templar saw, thankfully, that they were nearing her flat. What would he do now? Would he simply take Keri away from her or would he not carry out his threat to do so? Somehow Templar knew he was a man of his word, and that her agreement to his plans wasn't necessary to him. She hadn't meant it just now when she had said she wouldn't marry him to keep Keri, it just wasn't true. She had been willing to marry Ken to keep her, and she was just as willing to marry this cold hard stranger for the same reason.

Without being given directions he had driven straight to her tiny flat, following her into the house where she collected Keri from a smiling Mrs Street and carried the gurgling baby up to her own room. This was the time of day she loved best with the baby, when she could play with her for an hour or so, give her her bath, feed her, and then tuck her sleepily into her little cot. If she had carried on with her modelling career all this would have been left to a nanny, with her snatching the odd day with the baby in between travelling to assignments. Much as she loved this daily ritual with Keri it would have to wait a while this evening. Rather annoyingly Keri seemed to have taken a liking to the tall man with her 'Mama', holding out her arms to him to be held. Templar thrust her into his arms, turning away tearfully as Keri gave him her angelic smile and received a softening of those harsh features in return.

'Excuse me,' she said huskily. 'I'll just go and put the kettle on.' She fled into the kitchen before she made an absolute fool of herself. Close together like that there had been little doubt about their family likeness, and in a way Templar thought it unfair that Keri should have none of her mother's fair looks at all. Poor Tiffany, who had given her life for that small precious bundle of fun gurgling so happily in the arms of her aunt's greatest enemy.

Oh God, how she cursed herself for ever writing that letter! She should have waited for a few months, seen if things improved in any way. Instead her impetuous nature had led her into even greater unhappiness.

'Templar?'

She didn't turn, trying unsuccessfully to erase the tears from her cheeks. She felt herself gently turned round and she shivered slightly at the touch of his firm brown hands on her shoulders. Instantly they were removed. She looked at him through a sea of tears, flinching at the grim look in his now slate-grey eyes.

He forced up her chin. 'Now stop this, Templar, it is unnecessary. And it spoils your beauty.'

She gave a tremulous smile at his gentle tone. 'I thought that had already been spoilt.'

He turned away. 'I have never denied your beauty, as I have never denied that Keri is like you in every way. Keri?' he queried sharply. 'Is this not a strange name?'

'It's short for Kerina,' Templar explained, although she thought this an even more unusual name. Tiffany had chosen it herself during the few hours of life she had left to her after the birth of her daughter. Templar had never questioned it, but in the way that often happens the name had soon become shortened to Keri, and now she couldn't imagine that little squirming mass of fun being called anything else.

'Are you sure?' he asked shortly.

'Of course I'm sure.' What a silly question! Did he imagine she didn't even know the baby's name? 'Why?' she asked curiously, sensing that it meant something to him.

He shrugged his wide shoulders. 'It was my mother's name. Alex loved her very much.' A new respect entered his eyes. 'And I think he must have loved you very much too for him to have told you about her. It is not something he would have told a mere——'

'Mistress?' Templar supplied sweetly. 'But what makes you think he *did* tell me about her? I might have just chosen that name at random.'

He shook his head. 'It is hardly likely. It is too unusual for it to be so.'

Templar was inclined to agree with him. Tiffany had been adamant about the baby's name and at the time she had been too ill for Templar to enquire why. And a few hours later she had died. But Alex must have told her about his mother, there could be no other explanation. Could Templar have possibly misjudged him? But no, his brother had admitted that Alex had a fiancée, that he was to have been married only a month after he died. No, Alex Marcose must have been as she had imagined him to be, a young boy out for fun. And Tiffany had been that fun. Poor Tiffany, to give her beautiful young life through the selfishness of such a boy.

'What are you thinking about now?' Leondro Marcose demanded arrogantly.

'I was thinking that I will marry you after all. But on one condition.'

His head flicked back haughtily. 'I hardly think you are in a position to make conditions, do you?'

Templar shrugged her shoulders. 'That's up to you, of course. But my condition is this—I will not be pushed off into the background of your life as if you're ashamed of me. If that's the case then I think the baby and myself will be better off without you. If we're to be man and wife then I at least insist that we live in the same house.'

'You will insist on nothing! You will do as you are told! You know as well as I that we have no desire to share the same house.' His eyes narrowed suspiciously. 'Or have you decided to try your womanly charms on me after all?'

'Certainly not!' Templar blushed a fiery red at his wrong conclusion to her plan. She merely hoped he would change his mind about marrying her and simply look after her and the baby instead. 'That was the last thought on my mind. But if we're marrying to provide a stable home for Keri I do think it would be better— for her—if her mother and father lived together. Or do you intend to be a shadowy figure who appears in her life every six months or so and showers her with gifts?'

'That was not my intention. But neither was it my intention to live with you. You must see that it is impossible.'

Oh, she did, only too well—that was the whole point. 'Then I'm afraid the idea of marriage is impossible too. It just wouldn't work any other way. What could I say to Keri when she's older and wants to know why we live apart? That's almost as cruel as not having a father at all, crueller in some ways.'

'Good God, you talk as if the situation you find yourself in was *my* fault!'

'And isn't it? Isn't it? Alex was *your* brother. Didn't

he do exactly what you would have done in the same position? Didn't he?' she demanded.

He held himself stiffly. 'I have never refused to face up to my responsibilities, and neither has Alex. He would have provided for you if you had informed him of your—condition.'

'And if I didn't want his charity?'

'Then you were a very stubborn as well as stupid girl. But no matter, I regret I cannot live with you.'

'Oh, don't regret it,' Templar said smugly. 'I thought that might be your answer, and in the circumstances I can't marry you. If you choose to take me to court about the baby's guardianship that's up to you, but I'll fight it. Oh yes, I'll fight it! I don't think you would like the publicity any more than I would.'

'Perhaps not, but I would win.'

'Naturally,' she admitted. 'But would you like to put Keri through all that?'

'Would you? Oh, very well! We will share a house. It will have to be near London, I have too many business ties here to live anywhere else.' He looked impatiently angry at her blackmail.

Templar was dumbstruck, her plan backfiring on her. She hadn't expected this. She had thought he would drop his ideas of marriage and instead she had made matters worse. She would now have to share a home with this man. She shuddered at the thought of it. 'Um——' she hesitated. 'Perhaps—perhaps you were right. We—we could live apart.'

'No, *you* are right. Keri needs both parents.'

Templar felt a sick sinking feeling in her stomach. What had she let herself in for now?

CHAPTER THREE

TEMPLAR relaxed back on the garden lounger, smiling happily as Keri crawled about at her feet. They spent most of their afternoons like this and already, after only a few weeks, the two of them were attaining a healthy glow that had been sadly lacking. To Keri the huge garden was like a forest, and she loved nothing better than exploring its green depths.

It was three weeks since Templar's quiet wedding to Leondro Marcose, or Leon as she now called him. Not that they were any more friendly towards one another, but she could hardly address her own husband as Mr Marcose. Mrs Harvey, the housekeeper Leon had engaged, would have found that very odd, even odder than their sleeping arrangements. Leon's bedroom certainly adjoined her own, but the door between them was firmly locked and she could only assume that Leon had the key; she had certainly never seen it.

She had won the argument about not employing a nanny for Keri, although as a compromise she had agreed to a young girl being employed to help in her care. She couldn't possibly resent Lucy's shy offers of help and so the two of them managed very well. Luckily Keri liked her new playmate too.

And so everything ran smoothly and efficiently and Templar could almost have been happy if it weren't for her unwanted husband. He would never say anything to her, but she was always conscious of his silent disapproval of her. She was well aware that he only tolerated her at all because she had proved, in fact more than proved, that she was a good mother. And even Leondro Marcose couldn't deny the baby's love for her.

She watched Keri as she crawled over the flower-beds, her tiny body suitably clad in denim dungarees and a white tee-shirt. She didn't think Leon particularly approved of his 'daughter' wearing such clothes, but as yet he had made no comment. Templar glanced apprehensively at her wrist-watch. It was almost time for Leon to arrive home, the time she disliked the most.

A slight movement near the house caught and held her attention, and she found herself tensing as her husband shortened the distance between them with long easy strides. But her eyes passed on to the tall willowy blonde at his side, her hand resting possessively in the crook of his arm as she laughed provocatively up into his deeply tanned face.

Templar stood up, self-consciously smoothing down her creased denims and the white tee-shirt that matched the one Keri was now smearing with dirt. The baby laughed gleefully as her beloved 'Dadda' picked her up in his arms and swung her round, laughing uproariously at the pleasure in her tiny heart-shaped face.

She watched the two of them with fascination. With Keri, Leon was a completely different man, showing a side of his nature that Templar had never dreamt existed. He walked towards her now, Keri still in his arms, and the blonde girl still at his side. As they drew closer Templar had to suppress her gasp of recognition as she had a better view of the woman beside her husband. Rachel Winter!

The girl's blue eyes widened slightly as she also recognised Templar. 'Why, Templar darling,' she drawled huskily. 'What are you doing here? Surely you aren't darling Leon's little nanny?'

Templar blushed a furious red. She and Rachel had never been friends. Winter by name and wintry by nature, that was Rachel, except in the company of a handsome man, and then she purred like a satisfied cat. 'No, Rachel, I'm not Leon's nanny,' she replied coolly, looking pointedly towards her husband.

Leon stopped tickling the baby's toes long enough to look at the two women. 'Templar is my wife, Rachel. I thought you realised this.'

'Your wife?' Rachel's blue eyes narrowed chillingly. 'Templar is? I know you said you were married, darling, but I didn't realise that it was to Templar. I didn't even realise you knew her,' she smiled slightly. 'But by the look of that beautiful baby in your arms I would say you've known her for quite some time. So this is why you suddenly disappeared, Templar!'

Leon looked at them enquiringly. 'How do the two of you know each other?'

'Why, we're both models, darling,' Rachel laughed again, and Templar wondered if it was only because of her dislike of her that she thought the humour didn't reach this beautiful girl's eyes. 'At least, we were,' she amended. 'Are you aware that you've stolen one of the world's most sought-after models? Not that I mind, less competition for me.'

'You have no need to worry about competition,' Leon put in smoothly. 'You are very beautiful.' He smiled gratefully at Lucy as she brought out a tray containing three glasses of ice-cold lemonade. He handed Keri to the young girl. 'Please take the little one for her bath now. Her mother and I will be up to see her presently.' He sat down between the two women, handing them each a glass in turn. 'I have told Mrs Harvey that there will be one extra for dinner this evening, Templar. You will be staying, of course, Rachel?'

The model crossed one perfect leg over the other. 'That would be lovely, Leon. But don't let me interrupt your role of domesticity, Templar. I'm sure this lovely husband of yours and I can find plenty to talk about.'

Templar awoke from her dream world at the dismissal in the other girl's tone. She might only be here on sufferance, but she would not be made to look a fool in her own home. What part did Rachel play in Leon's life? And if it was the one Templar thought it was then he had no right to bring her here. Putting up with the company of his mistress was not part of their bargain. 'It's the usual practice for Lucy to bath Keri,' she said chillingly, glaring angrily at Leon. He had insisted that Lucy take over this duty and also be on call if Keri woke in the night, much to her chagrin.

'I see.' Rachel sipped appreciatively at the lemonade, the hot weather too much for her to face alcohol this early in the day. 'I was sorry to hear about Tiffany,' she added.

Templar stiffened, glancing nervously at Leon. Rachel could have no idea of the explosive subject she had just introduced to their conversation. 'Thank you,' she answered quietly. Oh God! She would have to change the subject quickly, she couldn't have Leon becoming suspicious about Tiffany. 'I thought those photographs of you taken in Africa were marvellous,' she said hurriedly. 'Really superb. Neil Adams was the photographer, wasn't he?'

'Mm.' Rachel visibly preened under the sincere admiration. 'He's really excellent. Actually, Tiffany was booked to do those photographs, but she backed out at the last minute. I think that must have been when she became ill.'

Leon was watching them through narrowed eyes and Templar shifted uncomfortably. 'Yes—yes, I remember now.' Tiffany had had to cancel that engagement because her waistline was starting to thicken and she hadn't wanted anyone to guess at her condition.

'What was actually wrong with her?' Rachel inquired. 'I heard that she'd died, but no one seemed to know why.'

Templar knew she was pale now, but she couldn't hide her distress, distress the other girl knew she must be causing when talking about her sister's death. It had been quite a few months since anyone had dared to mention Tiffany's death; the memory of it was still painful to her. What had made it all the more hurtful was the fact that they only had each other, their parents having died three years earlier in a pile-up on a motorway. With only a year difference in their ages the two girls had always been close, even closer after the double tragedy.

'She was—she was ill for several months before she died,' she explained breathlessly.

'Yes, but *what* did she die of?' Rachel persisted.

Templar sought about desperately in her mind for an answer. She could hardly reveal that Tiffany had died giving birth to Keri, that would make everything she had done so far just a waste of time. 'I—er—she——'

'I hope you will excuse us, Rachel,' Leon put in smoothly. 'My wife and I will have to go and say goodnight to the baby. Will you be all right while we go and see our daughter?'

'Yes, fine, darling.' Rachel stretched sensuously like a cat. 'But hurry back, won't you?'

Leon took Templar's arm firmly in his grip as they entered the house together, leading her to her bedroom and not to the nursery as she had expected. He sat her down in the bedroom chair, pinning her to the spot with those piercing blue-grey eyes of his, more grey now with his harsh mood. 'Now,' he began ominously, 'I want to know who Tiffany is.'

'Was,' she corrected him automatically. 'She—she was a friend of mine.'

'A very close friend, by the sound of it,' he snapped.

'All right,' she sighed, standing up agitatedly. 'She was a very close friend. Are you satisfied now?'

'No, I am not!' he said harshly. 'My brother knew a girl called Tiffany. What happened? Did you pass on your boy-friends from one girl to another?'

Templar paled even more. So Alex had mentioned Tiffany to his brother. It was something she had never thought of, Leon not appearing the sort of man to listen to tales of another's conquests. She would have to go very carefully from now on or she would trip herself up. 'No, we didn't! It's hardly any of my business if Tiffany and your brother went out together a few times,' she rounded on him angrily. 'But would you mind telling me why you brought that—that *woman* here? Or do you usually entertain your mistresses in your home? Because if you do I would prefer for the arrangements to be altered. Perhaps you could take her to your apartment. You may not care about the servants gossiping here, but I certainly do!'

The silence was nerve-racking after her outburst, the only sign that he had heard her at all was the pulse jerking erratically at his jawline. Her nerves tautened even more as the silence continued.

Finally he spoke. 'So you believe Rachel is my mistress?' he bit out angrily, his hands clenched into fists at his side. 'And on what evidence do you base this belief?'

'You sound like a lawyer,' Templar returned shrilly. 'I don't need evidence, Leon. I think your relationship is perfectly obvious. She certainly didn't come here to see me,' she laughed without humour. 'She didn't even realise I was your wife. I suppose I should feel grateful that she even knew you had a wife, even if she did think I was the nanny.'

'That is hardly surprising, is it!' he said viciously. 'You have the look of a virginal innocent which is totally deceiving. Many women would have taken Rachel's mistake as a compliment.'

'I'm not many women! And it wasn't meant as a compliment. I've known her too long to be deceived by that sweet sugary smile of hers. She was just trying to make me feel small. And she succeeded,' she added dryly.

To her surprise Leon smiled, or as near as he had come to smiling at her since he had returned home from work. 'You have no need to feel small. And I am perfectly well aware of Rachel's faults.' His face hardened again. 'But I will not allow you to say she is my mistress, it is just not true. She was a friend of Alex's.'

'Another one!' she burst out. My, that boy certainly seemed to have got around!

He nodded. 'Another one,' he echoed sadly.

'But now she's your—friend, right?'

'Wrong!' he snapped. 'Rachel has been working mainly abroad the last year or so and had no opportunity to offer her regrets at Alex's death. I could do little other than offer our hospitality in the circumstances, especially as it became apparent that the two of you know each other.'

'You don't have to explain yourself to me,' Templar muttered stiffly. 'I merely requested that you don't bring your mistresses here. Is that too much to ask?'

'Rachel is not my mistress!' Leon took a threatening step towards her. 'And you will please be more polite about a guest in your own home.'

'This isn't my home, I'm merely granted permission to stay here! I'm tolerated if you like. But you can't force me to be polite to *your* guest. I don't like Rachel Winter, I never have done.'

'Do not be childish!'

'But I am, aren't I?' She felt the frustration of being treated like a guest in her own home the last few weeks well up inside her. 'You treat me like a stranger, you hardly speak to me, you never spend time with me! How can I be other than childish when a child is all I have to talk to all day?' Her voice broke on a sob. 'I hate it here. I hate it!'

Her husband held himself haughtily erect, looking down at her bent head. 'You knew what it would be like when you married me, when you forced us to live together like this. As to your having no one to talk to, you have Mrs Harvey and Lucy.'

'Oh, yes!' Her eyes sparkled angrily as she flicked back her long hair. 'To them I'm the mistress of this house, someone to whom they listen, but don't easily converse with. And to you I'm just an inferior. I had a baby without being married to her father, and in your eyes that makes me less than worthy of your esteemed attention——' she broke off as one long tanned hand flicked out to give her a resounding slap across one cheek. Her hand flew up to her face and she stared at him in horror, tears of pain welling up in her eyes.

'Oh God!' he swore angrily in his own language, grasping her forearms tightly as she tried to jerk away from him. 'I am sorry, so sorry.'

Templar shook her head, her cheek stinging painfully. 'No, you're not. Just let me go. Let me go!'

'No.' Leon's voice was deep with emotion. 'Please, Templar! You were saying things that just aren't true and it was the only way I knew to quieten you—well, perhaps not the only way. But I think you would have liked my other method even less.'

'Wh—what other method?' she sobbed.

'I have found that kissing also stops hysteria. But I think in our case it might have made things worse.' He tilted her chin gently with his fingers. 'Smile, Templar. Come, smile for me. Or if not for me, for yourself. You are much too beautiful to upset yourself like this.'

Templar wiped away the tears, tears of shock more than pain, attempting a tremulous smile. 'I'm sorry. I'm not usually so—so emotional.'

'And I am not usually such a brute. But perhaps you should be more emotional,' he said gently. 'You have had much to be emotional about the last year or so and it is better not to repress these feelings.' He moved away from her. 'Now, are you ready to say goodnight to our little one?'

Templar nodded, smoothing back her hair. 'I must look a mess,' she said ruefully.

He wiped a tear away that had escaped his attentions earlier and strangely she found his touch pleasant. 'Never a mess, Templar. You are much too beautiful to ever look anything else. And you are puzzling too.'

'I—I am?' She glanced at him quickly. 'But why?'

Leon studied her thoughtfully. 'You are something of an enigma. One moment I think I know exactly who and what you are and the next moment I am forced to revise my opinion of you completely. What are you, Templar—innocence or experience?'

She forced a confident laugh, the mark of his hand starting to fade from her hot cheek. 'A bit of both, I suppose. I have Keri to prove one of them and I'm afraid you'll have to take my word for the other.'

She saw his face stiffen and the coldness re-enter his

eyes until they were that deep grey colour that she hated. But she had to keep him hating her, because she had a feeling that if he should ever change his mind about disliking her she would find it hard to resist him! Very rarely had she seen the charm he could exert, but it had been enough to know that any woman he desired would stand little chance against him. But she would! What was the matter with her anyway? She hated this man, didn't she? Hated what his brother had done to her sister?

'If you are quite in control of yourself now,' Leon's words were stilted, 'we will go in to see Keri.'

Templar didn't bother to answer him, the coldness entering their relationship that had been the normal pattern of their days since their wedding. She walked into the nursery adjoining her room, instantly hearing Keri's contented chuckles. Straight away the sound brought a smile to her face. To see the baby so happy was worth being married to a man she didn't love, could never love, and who would never love her. As long as Keri never had to want for anything again she could bear to live with this cold hard stranger who was her husband.

She took the willing Keri from Lucy's arms, dismissing the girl with a smile. 'Hello, poppet. Have you been a good girl?'

Leon came to stand at her side and Templar thought that anyone looking at the three of them would have thought them ecstatically happy. How wrong they would be!

As usual the baby glowed when in the company of her now favourite person. It had hurt at first to realise she now took second place to Leon in her daughter's affections, but it was something that couldn't be helped. Keri adored this man who had suddenly appeared in her life, as he surely adored her. To see the two of them together one could almost imagine that Leon *was* her father.

Keri put her chubby little arms out towards Leon. 'Da-Da, Dada,' she gurgled.

Templar sensed rather than saw his probing look in her direction as he took the baby into his arms. 'Did you teach her to say that?' he asked tautly.

She couldn't tell whether his mood was angry or otherwise and she moved nervously under his intent look. 'I—I—Yes, I did!' She held her head up defiantly.

'Thank you,' was all he said in reply.

Templar turned away, a huge lump in her throat. His tautness hadn't been due to anger at all but because he was actually moved by Keri's chatter. 'Would you—' she hesitated. 'Would you like to put her to bed while I change for dinner? I won't be long,' she promised.

She was determined that Rachel Winter shouldn't outdo her. One of the first things Leon had insisted on doing was to buy her lots of new clothes, and she had decided to wear one of the new gowns to dinner this evening.

'You go ahead,' he said quietly. 'And please—be polite to Rachel. That is not too much to ask, is it?'

She shook her head. 'No, I suppose not. And, Leon —I'm sorry.' His eyebrows rose enquiringly. 'For acting like a bitchy wife,' she explained. 'It isn't like me at all. In fact, I'm not used to acting like any sort of wife. I think that's probably because I don't particularly feel married.'

'But you are,' he said sternly. 'Very much so.'

'Mm,' she tickled Keri under her chin, evading Leon's eyes. 'We have you to prove that, don't we, mischief?'

'As I told you, it has been easily accepted that Keri is my child,' Leon remarked coolly. 'No one is to know differently. And when she is old enough, we will explain to her that I am not her father. Only to Keri can it ever be important.'

And will we also explain that I'm not her mother? The question screamed out in Templar's mind. Keri would have to be told about Tiffany one day, she could not be kept in ignorance about her real mother. But by that time Keri should be old enough for it not to matter if Leon threw her 'mother' out.

'You're right,' she agreed. 'I'll just go and change and pop back in a few minutes to say goodnight to the baby.'

'Very well. I will put the little one to bed and then go downstairs and entertain our guest. We cannot leave her alone for too long. I will change myself when you come down.'

Templar took her time deciding which dress to wear, nothing too formal but then again nothing too *in*formal. She had to admit that anything would be an improvement on the denims and tee-shirt she was wearing. She finally settled on a thin woollen dress in a particularly lovely shade of moss green. Her choice was a good one, the green of the dress bringing out the pure auburn of her hair.

Leon and Rachel were deep in conversation when she arrived at the lounge, and her presence wasn't noticed for several long minutes. It gave her a chance to observe them without their being aware of it, and no matter what Leon said, Rachel did not appear to be just a friend of his brother. Far from it in fact; the beautiful blonde often touched his arm as she stressed certain points. Templar couldn't hear what they were saying, but it certainly wasn't an impersonal conversation.

'Good evening,' she said pointedly, before either of them noticed her and thought her to be eavesdropping. 'I hope I haven't kept you waiting.'

Leon stood up in one fluid movement, his eyes sliding insolently over her slim body as she squarely met those appraising eyes. It was the first time that he had acknowledged in any way that she was an attractive woman. Granted he had said she was beautiful, but it had been in a cold abrupt manner as if he were talking about the weather or something else equally impersonal. The look in his eyes now was one of a man who found her desirable.

He came forward and kissed her fleetingly on the forehead, tightly grasping her arms as she would have flinched away from him. 'May I say how lovely you are looking tonight, Templar?' His eyes were glacial as he silently warned her to behave herself. He took her arm and led her further into the room. 'Please entertain Rachel while I shower and change. I will not be long.'

Templar looked after him regretfully. What could she possibly talk to Rachel about? They had nothing in common, they never had. But it seemed that Rachel had no more desire to converse with Templar than she had with her, sitting back with a bored expression on her face. Occasionally she would attempt to stifle a yawn, and Templar found herself becoming more and more angry.

'So,' she burst out finally. 'What are you doing now?'

Rachel looked at her with contemptuous blue eyes. 'Working, of course. You must find it terrifically boring being at home all the time. Somehow I never pictured you in the devoted mother role.'

'I didn't realise you ever thought of me enough to visualise me in any role.' It seemed to her that Rachel only usually thought of herself.

Rachel smiled languidly. 'I don't, darling. But even so, it is quite surprising. Although I can't imagine Leon allowing his wife to do anything else but stay at home. You must have known Alex too—charming devil, wasn't he? But not as charming as his brother. Leon is perfect, isn't he? The absolute perfect male.'

'That happens to be my husband you're talking about, Rachel,' Templar reminded her stiffly.

'Oh, I know that. But that doesn't stop him being the fascinating man he is, and it doesn't stop him seeing me as a beautiful woman.' Rachel's smile was plainly smug.

'Just as modest as ever, I see,' said Templar dryly. 'You really are in the wrong profession, Rachel. With conceit like yours I'm sure you could have entered something much more lucrative than modelling.'

Rachel smiled slightly, her beautiful painted mouth pure perfection, and her make-up looking as fresh as if it had just been applied. 'I don't intend staying in modelling for ever. Oh no, Templar, I'm going to be clever like you and marry a rich man. How did you manage that, by the way? I can't imagine how you ever met Leon, you never came to any of those parties the rest of us attended looking for a rich husband.'

'I didn't need to look for Leon, he found me.' Which was true—he *had* found her, maybe not in the way Rachel meant, but he had found her.

'Really?' Rachel enquired sweetly. 'And how long have the two of you been married?'

'Not long enough,' remarked Leon as he came into the room, walking with long easy strides to Templar's side as if this was how they spent all their evenings. 'Have we, darling?' he smiled down at her.

Templar flushed under the taunting gaze of the other girl, attempting to smile at her husband. 'No, Leon, we haven't.' She knew Leon had said they were to put on an act in front of other people, but did he have to do it in front of this girl? Rachel was too shrewd to be taken in by an over-show of emotion. 'Was Keri asleep when you came down?'

'Mm,' Leon smiled the completely natural smile that always appeared when he thought of the baby. 'And looking beautiful, like her mother.'

She bowed her head. 'Thank you.'

'I only state the obvious,' he said more coolly. 'Shall we all go in to dinner now?'

Leon insisted on taking Rachel home later on in the evening and left Templar wondering why. Unless, as she had thought, Leon was more interested in the model than as just a friend of his brother. Strangely enough the idea was repugnant to her. If Leon had to have a mistress, as such a virile man as he must surely have, she dearly hoped it wouldn't be someone she knew, and especially not Rachel. The fact that he might be making love to an unknown woman somehow didn't make it real, but to actually know who it was would be too humiliating. And she could imagine Rachel's glee at putting her in such a position.

Templar was already in bed and trying to sleep when she heard the soft purr of the powerful engine of Leon's car. Almost one o'clock! It was over two hours since Leon had left to take Rachel home and it didn't take much imagination to know what had happened in the intervening time. She sat up in bed, dragging the bed-clothes up with her. How dared he! How dared he

bring that woman here and then spend a further two
hours in her company, alone! He was supposed to be
happily married!

She got angrily out of bed as she heard Leon's soft
firm tread in the adjoining bedroom, flinging on her
silk dressing-gown to march out into the corridor and
wrench open the door of his bedroom. She stood in the
doorway, her green eyes flashing angrily and her long
auburn tresses shimmering far down her back.

Leon looked up at her, his eyes narrowing question-
ingly. He was in the process of undressing, having discarded his jacket and partially unbuttoned his shirt,
showing the fine mat of dark hairs on his tanned chest.

He straightened. 'Did you want something, Templar, or is this a social call?'

Her eyes flashed and she advanced into the room,
uncaring of her sheer almost transparent clothing.
'Don't talk down to me like that, Leon,' she warned. 'I
won't have it! I asked you earlier if Rachel was your
mistress and you said she——'

'Was not,' he finished angrily. 'And she still is not!'
He was regarding her through eyes that flickered with
a strange emotion she didn't understand. 'What ridiculous notions have you conceived in that lovely young
head of yours? Do you imagine that I took home the
sophisticated Rachel, made wild passionate love to her,
and then calmly came back here? Is that what you
think?'

Templar held herself stiffly, her look defiant. 'And
why not? Or do you think yourself above such things?'

He gave a devilish grin before his face sobered again,
his blue-grey eyes becoming a steely grey. 'Oh, no,
Templar, I am not above such things. But if I make
love to a desirable woman it is not a thing to be rushed
and hidden from the world. And can you honestly see

Rachel dropping her beautiful façade enough to give her body in passion?' he shook his head decisively. 'I cannot. She is a beautiful mask, that one, and without that poise and sophistication she would be nothing. Besides, I am a married man.'

'You obviously don't know Rachel as well as I thought you did if you believe the little fact of your being married would deter her. Rachel is on the look-out for a rich protector if she can't find her own husband, and I think she has decided you would meet her requirements admirably.'

'And do I have no say in the matter?'

'Apparently not.'

'I see. And is this the reason you have come bursting into my bedroom in the early hours of the morning with fire in your eyes?' His mouth tightened ominously. 'Do you think it safe to enter the bedroom of a—an *animal*, in such a way? For that is what you think I am, is it not? A man who can behave as an animal and take his pleasures where he finds them?'

'No, I—' Templar shifted uncomfortably, realising he was blazingly angry with her. 'I didn't mean— I——'

'I know perfectly well what you meant, Templar. Now would you mind removing yourself from my bedroom, or are you waiting to see if I live up to your expectations?'

'Expectations?' she repeated, shivering as she pulled her wrap more closely around her slender body.

'Oh yes, you have made it perfectly obvious what you expect of me,' he snapped. 'Are you sure *you* feel safe in my company?'

Templar laughed nervously. 'You're mocking me.'

'Am I?' he asked softly.

'You know you are. You've never—well, you've

never made any—any advances towards me.'

Leon gave a harsh laugh. 'What do you think I am? You have borne my brother's child, I could no more touch you than I could stop breathing.'

'I—You——'

'Please, Templar, get out of here!' He ran an agitated hand through his thick dark hair. 'I don't know what you want, but I certainly cannot give it to you.'

'You—you swine! I didn't come in here for anything other than to tell you I thought your behaviour disgusting!'

'Really? Well, your opinion is not important to me, I live by my own rules.'

'And what about Keri?'

'What about her? She is well looked after, cosseted and deeply loved by all about her. Why should the fact that her "parents" do not love *each other* matter to her? Come, Templar, even though you did not love my brother surely you can see Keri is being brought up in the way he would have wished for her.'

'Of course I can!' she snapped. 'And I also told you that Keri was born out of love! Or have you forgotten?'

'I have not forgotten, I simply find it hard to believe you ever loved my brother. You are much more mature than Alex ever was.'

'And don't you think that having a baby and caring for that baby alone is enough to mature anyone?' Actually Tiffany had always been very young for her age, and that was why Templar blamed herself for not protecting her better. She had always cared for her younger sister, but in this she had failed.

A flicker of pain crossed his face. 'You know I would have helped you if I had known of your situation, even if Alex would not. It is against all that I believe to let you carry on alone.'

'So you married me,' Templar said bitterly. 'Poor Leon, prepared to go to any lengths to protect your family name. Even marry a girl you hardly knew, a girl moreover who isn't even sure that your brother was Keri's father.'

His face tightened. 'I wish you would not make remarks like that. I have told you that the baby's family resemblance is perfectly obvious, and if you cannot see it for yourself then you must be blind.'

'She does have a look of you about her,' she agreed thoughtfully.

'And Alex.' Leon gave her a hard glance.

'Well, of course Alex. That goes without saying,' she said swiftly.

'Why does it? She is not that much like Alex, only on certain occasions. Not all babies look like their parents, they often have the look of a close relative.'

She knew that. Oh yes, she definitely knew that! 'I realise that. But if Keri looks like you it automatically follows that she looks like Alex.' Didn't it? Oh God, she hoped so!

'I see.' He continued to unbutton what remained fastened of his shirt. 'Now if you have quite finished I wish to go to bed.'

'Oh—oh, of course.' She turned back to the door. 'I'm sorry for interrupting you.'

'That is perfectly all right. I hope now that you are satisfied I do not intend jumping into Rachel's bed either now or in the future. And you will please stop apologising. It does not suit you.'

'I'm sorry—oh!'

'Please just go, Templar,' Leon said wearily. 'I have had a long day and arguing with you is not my idea of relaxation.'

'I'm——' she broke off as she realised she was about to apologise yet again. 'Goodnight,' she murmured.

'Goodnight,' he echoed gently.

CHAPTER FOUR

TEMPLAR awoke the next day with a raging headache and a throbbingly sore throat. She sighed miserably. Wasn't it just typical that all during her months of deprivation she hadn't been ill once and now that she was living in the lap of luxury, so to speak, she had her old ailment, tonsillitis. She pulled herself feebly up the bed, making an effort to get up and dress herself. It was after eight and Keri would soon be screaming the house down, in fact she was surprised she hadn't already done so.

She collapsed back against the pillows, feeling too weak to move any further. How ridiculous she felt! To be made so weak just through a sore throat and a headache. She drifted drowsily back to sleep, only to wake with a start as a soft knock sounded on the door.

'Come in,' she called croakily.

Leon entered the room, a chuckling Keri in his arms. Templar subsided below the bedclothes, but her husband had no such thought for her modesty, coming to stand unconcernedly beside the bed.

'Good morning, Templar,' he greeted politely. 'Your daughter has been asking incessantly for her mama, and I really could not deprive her of your company another moment longer.'

'Hello, darling,' her voice was husky as she spoke to the baby. 'Has she been awake long?' she asked Leon. 'I don't usually sleep in this late.'

'I realise that, but it will not do you any harm for once. You must have been fast asleep when Keri woke

67

at seven o'clock. I have been doing my best to entertain her, but I am afraid that as far as Keri is concerned I make a poor substitute.'

Templar smiled slightly, taking Keri down with her on the bed. 'I'm sure that isn't true. Keri adores you and you know it.' Even to her own ears her voice sounded hoarse and she blushed as she saw Leon's questing look.

'Are you quite well?'

She smiled brightly, unaware of her flushed feverish features and slightly glazed eyes. 'I'm fine,' she assured him. 'Are you not going to work this morning?' She changed the subject, playing with Keri and her teddy bear.

'No. It is Saturday and I thought I would spend the day with my—family.' Leon took a closer look at her. 'You are not well,' he stated. 'I can see it is so, so do not attempt to deny it again. Why did you lie to me?'

'I didn't!' Her voice broke, confirming that she did. 'Anyway,' she bridled angrily, 'if this sudden decision to spend time with us is because of my outburst yesterday then you needn't have bothered. I'm afraid I became rather upset yesterday and said things I wouldn't have done normally.'

'But it was the truth, nevertheless,' he said stiffly, moving away from the bed to look out of the window. 'You were correct in saying I do not spend time with you and Keri and it is something I intend to rectify.'

'Please!' Templar put up a weary hand. 'We don't —at least, I don't, want your forced friendliness. If you want to be with the baby then please go ahead. But don't include me in any of your plans. I can find plenty to amuse me.'

'Do not be childish! It is something I have noticed that you do a lot when you are most annoyed or hurt.

Which one is it today?'

'Neither,' she dismissed, really feeling too ill to bandy words with such a steely opponent. 'I'm just not in the mood to act the delighted wife at her husband's belated attentions. Fortunately, Keri doesn't seem to have the same reservations, so I'm sure she will be over-joyed to be taken out by her beloved Dadda.'

'You will not come with us?'

Templar shook her head and then wished she hadn't. The pounding in her head had become a sharp digging pain and all she wanted to do was go back to sleep until she felt better. 'No,' she snuggled beneath the covers. 'I'm feeling sleepy this morning. If you're going to take Keri out I may as well stay here and have a lie in. Do you mind?' she asked, not really caring how he felt one way or the other.

'Not if that is what you would prefer to do,' Leon said haughtily, his eyes glacial. 'I am sure the little one and I will entertain each other very well.' He picked Keri up from the bed. 'We will see you later. Sleep well.'

'I will,' she replied tiredly, already half asleep.

She didn't wake until late into the afternoon, rousing herself drowsily as she heard a movement in the bed-room. Her eyes flew open to meet the steely grey ones of her husband. 'H—hello,' she said weakly.

'I have brought you some tea.' He looked down at her distantly. 'You have been asleep a long time. I did not realise you had become as tired as this.'

Templar looked at him suspiciously but could read little from his expression. 'Are you being sarcastic?' she asked bluntly.

He raised a surprised eyebrow at her tone before his firm well-shaped mouth curved into a slight smile. 'No, Templar. I am not being sarcastic. You are very forthright in the way you speak.' He moved forward slightly, and Templar saw that he was dressed in close-fitting black trousers and a maroon-coloured shirt that fitted tautly across his chest and showed a fine mat of dark hair at its open neckline.

Even though she was feeling ill she could appreciate that Leon was a breathtakingly handsome man, the sort of man she never imagined marrying.

'Is caring for Keri too much for you?' he continued. 'You know that I wanted you to be free of this constant demand on your time and energy. But you would not have it,' he finished in disgust.

Her eyes became feverish and her face flushed as she struggled angrily into a sitting position, uncaring of her state of undress, and unaware of the attractive picture she made in the green shimmering nightdress that exactly matched her eyes and complemented the long auburn tresses down her slender back. 'Of course I wouldn't have it,' she flared. 'Keri is *my* child, I *want* to give my time and energy to her. She's all I have in the world.'

He frowned deeply. 'That is not strictly true. You have me too now, or had you forgotten?'

Templar shook her head, smoothing her damp hair off her hot forehead. 'I haven't forgotten you, but this marriage hardly matters, does it? As soon as Keri is old enough to understand I'll no longer be necessary and you'll be able to be free of me.'

Leon strode forward angrily. 'Why do you persist in these ridiculous thoughts? I——'

'Please, Leon,' she begged weakly, 'don't start to lecture me now. I—I don't feel like being treated as a child today.' She ran a hand over her aching eyes. 'I just want to go back to sleep and never wake up. My head aches, my throat aches, my body feels like a heavy weight's been dropped on it, and I—I—' her lips trembled and the tears began to fall softly down her cheeks. 'Oh, Leon, I feel—I feel *awful*!'

For a moment he continued to look at her uncertainly and then as if he had fought a battle with himself and won, he came forward and pulled her roughly against his chest as she continued to cry softly. 'Why did you not say so, you silly child?' He placed her back against the pillows. 'A doctor must be called for you immediately.' He removed her hands from around his neck and effectively moved away from her. 'I will not be long,' he promised.

Templar watched him leave the room through tear-wet eyes. Poor Leon, how he must hate having to show concern for someone he despised. But she *was* feeling ill. It certainly wasn't just tonsillitis as she had first thought, although goodness knows that could be painful enough. Ever since she was a child she had had intermittent outbreaks of the infection, and for a couple of days it made her feel absolutely terrible.

True to his word Leon called the doctor straight away and within half an hour the kindly man had confirmed her suspicions that she had 'flu.

'Although,' continued the doctor sternly, a dark disapproving look on his face as he looked at Leon Marcose, 'it isn't only 'flu your wife is suffering from. The complaint is made worse by her complete mental and physical exhaustion. I suppose, like most husbands, you haven't realised what a strain caring for a baby, a husband, and a home too can put on a young girl. But I hope you realise that your wife is very delicate.'

'Yes, I realise this,' Leon replied stiffly, unused to people talking to him in this way but accepting the man's superior knowledge about such things. 'So, what do you advise?'

'When your wife is sufficiently recovered from this virus I think it would be advisable for you to get her away to a warmer climate for a well-earned holiday.'

'Oh, but I—' gasped Templar. 'I don't want to go on holiday,' she declared.

Leon looked down at her coldly. 'It has been suggested and I therefore intend to make the arrangements. You are in no fit state to argue the point. Rest now and we will talk later.'

'But——'

'Now then, young lady,' the doctor interrupted sternly, 'you must do as you're told. Your husband and I know what's best for you.' He indicated that they should leave the room as her eyelids began to droop tiredly.

Leon closed the door quietly behind him. 'You are sure this is what my wife needs?' he queried politely.

'Yes, I'm sure,' the doctor confirmed. 'Your wife needs a long rest, she has little resistance to infection at the moment. A holiday away from her normal environment might be the extra tonic she needs.'

'I see,' said Leon slowly. 'And what of the baby? I do not think Templar would be willing to leave her here.'

The doctor gave him a strange look. 'I don't think that will be necessary. Your wife is obviously very attached to your child and to part them would only worsen her condition.' He quickly wrote out a prescription and handed it to the man at his side. 'See that your wife takes these. And see that she rests for the next few days—not that she's going to feel much like being energetic, but you know how these young mothers are. No one can look after their child as they can.'

For the first time the younger man smiled. 'In that I

am in total agreement with you. I am afraid Templar insists on doing almost everything for the baby,' he shook his dark head. 'And my wife can be very determined when she sets her mind on something.'

The two men laughed companionably as they walked down the stairs, although the doctor found the relationship between this couple faintly puzzling. Although he hadn't been especially observant it had been apparent to the most casual of glances that husband and wife occupied separate bedrooms. He shrugged his shoulders—these modern marriages! It wouldn't do for Peggy and himself. Thirty years they had been married now and not once had they occupied separate rooms, except during the birth of their two children, of course.

He smiled at the other man. 'Mrs Marcose will need plenty of fluids over the next few days, but if she doesn't feel like eating I shouldn't worry too much. I'll call back in a couple of days' time, but call me before if you think she's worse.'

Leon saw him to the door himself, the smile fading from his harsh features as soon as the door was closed.

Templar raised herself on one elbow to watch the baby as she crawled about on the deep-pile carpet, revelling in its softness beneath her touch. Lucy had brought Keri in for a short time on Templar's instructions. This was her fourth day in bed and quite frankly she was getting tired of it. The doctor had been back once and confirmed that she was progressing nicely. At the time she had been feeling too ill to care, but she was feeling slightly better today and didn't see why she shouldn't see the baby for a short time. Keri had been overjoyed to see her again, although she didn't let her too close, not wanting Keri to catch the infection.

She smiled gratefully at the young nursemaid. 'I

hope you haven't found it too tiring these last few days looking after Keri. I know what a handful she can be at times.' She laughed as Keri's serious green eyes looked at her enquiringly. 'Yes, imp, I'm talking about you. What a little monkey you are!'

'She's been very good while you've been ill, Mrs Marcose. And of course your husband had been with her for quite a lot of the time,' Lucy explained.

Templar's face became a shuttered mask at the mention of Leon. She had seen little of him, although she knew he was spending more time at home at the moment. As far as she knew he enquired as to her condition each day, but she had only seen him once herself, and that had only been when he had accompanied the doctor to her room for the second time, and then it had only been for a very short time.

For some reason Leon seemed to be avoiding seeing her. Unless he was otherwise occupied! Although he had denied an affair with Rachel that didn't mean he wasn't seeing someone else. Surely he was too much of a man to be completely without a woman in his life, a woman he could share a physical relationship with.

She brought her thoughts up sharply as she saw Lucy's concerned look, smiling brightly at the younger girl. 'As long as Keri has behaved that's all that matters.'

In a way she found it quite hurtful that Keri accepted these strangers so easily into her young life. It felt strange after being the centre of the baby's world to suddenly find herself so easily replaced, strange and just a little frightening. If Keri became too independent of her love Leon might consider she was no longer necessary. Her heart constricted painfully at the thought and her face paled. She couldn't lose Keri, she just couldn't!

Lucy saw her suddenly strained face and picking up Keri from the floor she walked over to the door. 'I think I should take Keri back to her room now, it's almost time for her nap anyway.'

'And mine,' laughed Templar. 'Don't worry, Lucy, I'm not going to have a relapse. I'll be up and about again in a couple of days and able to relieve you of some of Keri's care.'

'I've been fine, honestly.'

'I know,' Templar nodded. 'But if the truth be known I miss the little bundle of mischief.' She cleared the slight catch in her throat. 'Very much,' she added softly.

She stared sightlessly at the ceiling after Lucy had left with the baby. She would go mad if she had to spend much more time in this room on her own. But the doctor had said she had to stay in bed another few days. Well, she wouldn't! She wouldn't stay here a moment longer. Perhaps if Leon had made some effort to see her she might have suffered this convalescence, but not if she was going to be kept here out of the way like something he could forget existed if she was out of sight. Well, she wasn't going to be out of sight much longer!

She swung her long legs over the side of the bed, pushing the restricting covers back irritably. She would get up for lunch and surprise Leon. It would certainly surprise him! He must imagine he was almost a bachelor again. She would soon disillusion him about that.

She put her feet firmly on the floor and pushed herself up. Goodness, her legs felt terribly wobbly! And the bathroom door suddenly seemed very far away.

It seemed to take her an age to reach the pale blue door, but she finally got there, clasping on to the door handle as if it were a lifeline. Perhaps this wasn't such a good idea after all. But, oh dear, it seemed to be an even longer way back. She swayed on her feet, her head swimming dizzily. It was no good, she would have to get back to the bed. She wouldn't be able to dress herself, let alone present herself before Leon as a healthy young woman.

Perhaps if she held on to the stool in front of the dressing-table and then moved on to the wardrobe she might be able to get back that way. It was a longer way back to the bed than just walking straight across the room, but it seemed safer in the long run.

She made the small distance to the stool, but the wardrobe suddenly seemed very far away and it took her a few minutes to get the strength together to make the second effort. Well, it was now or never; she couldn't stay here all day and she certainly wasn't going to call out for Leon. That would be too humiliating.

She took one hesitant step forward, only to feel herself losing her balance, the floor coming towards her fast. The stool fell over with a clatter and Templar landed with a loud thud beside it. Tears of indignation welled up in her stricken eyes and she gazed sorrowfully at the door, waiting inevitably for someone to arrive. It was too much to hope that no one had heard the noise.

Her instincts were correct and a couple of second later Leon came bursting into the room. He took in the situation at a glance, dismissing the staff who had gathered around the doorway, coming down on his haunches beside Templar as she looked away from him.

'What happened?' he demanded.

She still couldn't look at him, although she tried to wipe away the tears of frustration that still stood on her flushed cheeks. 'I fell over,' she whispered.

'I realise that,' Leon returned tersely, grasping her forearms to pull her to her feet. He swung her effortlessly up into his arms, holding her tightly against his chest. 'What I want to know is what you were doing out of bed in the first place. You know you were supposed to stay in bed for another few days. Doctor's orders,' he said firmly.

Templar quivered against him, completely unnerved by the warmth exuded by his body so close to her own. The tears still shimmered in her eyes, spilling over and falling down her cheeks as she looked down at the open neck of his tan-coloured shirt. A fine mat of dark hairs could be seen there and she looked away again quickly. 'Please don't be cross with me, Leon,' she pleaded softly. 'Please!'

The dark head bent and a pair of grey-blue eyes looked intently down at her. Templar blushed under that searching gaze, looking back at him shyly, aware of her auburn hair splayed out across his chest. 'I was not going to be cross with you,' Leon denied gently. 'I merely wondered why you had been so silly as to get out of bed against the doctor's wishes—and mine, I might add.'

'I realise it was against yours,' she said quietly, adding nothing more.

'What do you mean?' he frowned.

'I know you don't like to be reminded of my existence, but I just couldn't stay up here on my own another moment longer. It's so lonely.'

For a long moment he was silent, still holding her tightly against him. 'I—' he hesitated. 'I have never said I wished you did not exist, on the contrary, if you did not exist then neither would Keri, and you know how we both love her. Indeed, I am very grateful to you for giving me such a beautiful child.'

'But you—you haven't been to see me at all, except when you accompanied the doctor,' she accused.

He raised a dark eyebrow. 'Did you want me to? If I remember correctly you professed a wish for me not to bother you with my belated attentions.'

'You know you remember correctly!' she said hotly. 'But you should also remember that I wasn't feeling well at the time and obviously said things I didn't mean.'

Leon grinned down at her. 'What you said that day did not seem so very different from what you usually say. I have become used to you scolding me. I have not visited you because I did not want to upset you as I usually seem to do when I come near you.'

She looked at him suspiciously. 'Was that the only reason? I know you don't like me, but I——'

'Templar!' he snapped warningly, placing her gently on the bed and pulling the covers up over her thinly clad body as she ineffectually tried to do so herself. He sat down on the side of the bed. 'I have never said such a thing. You have a way of putting words into my mouth that is totally false. I have explained why I have not been up to see you, but if it will please you I will sit with you for a while. Would you like that?'

'Mm,' she nodded her head shyly. 'If you're sure I'm not keeping you from something else——'

'Not some*thing* or some*one*,' Leon interrupted, standing up to bring her bedroom chair next to the bed. 'Now tell me how you are feeling?'

'I'm all right now, thank you, Leon.' She laughed slightly, a catch in her throat. 'And to think I was going to come downstairs and show you how well I am!'

'Now I can see how well you are here. I have made the arrangements for our holiday and——'

'Holiday!' burst out Templar. 'I told you I didn't want to go on holiday.'

'And I told you that we *were* going,' her husband insisted. 'And you know that I always have my own way in such things.'

'You're very arrogant, Leon,' she said tartly. 'It isn't something that I desired in a husband.'

He grinned at her again. 'I am sorry if it does not please you. I have always been so.'

'Well, it isn't something to be proud of,' reprimanded Templar, wondering at her own audacity. 'And I still say I won't go on this holiday. I couldn't leave Keri.'

'I informed the doctor of this and I am afraid he was rather shocked by my even thinking he meant us to leave the baby behind. I think I shocked his sensibilities,' Leon chuckled wryly. 'I should have remembered that the English very rarely leave the care of their children to other people. Your reaction to my suggestion of a nanny for Keri should have been enough to remind me.'

'Surely you wouldn't like to leave her behind? I'm sure you would find it rather tiresome to entertain me.'

Leon's eyes darkened to a deep blue, his look unreadable in its intensity. 'I would not have found it tiresome at all. On the contrary, it may have proved— interesting.'

She looked away in confusion. 'And now?'

'Now we are taking the baby with us.'

'Where will we be going?'

'I have a villa in France. It will do admirably for our needs. A couple are in residence there all the year round and they take care of my needs when I go there. Lucy can accompany us to help in the caring of the baby. I am sure Keri will enjoy her holiday enormously, she has a way of enjoying everything.'

For the first time since Leon had entered her bedroom Templar smiled confidently. 'She's a very happy child. And she's much more contented since we've lived here.'

'Since you married me,' Leon corrected. 'No matter how much you try to forget it I am afraid it is an inescapable fact.'

'Did you have to get on to that subject?' she cut in shortly. 'I was quite enjoying our little chat, and now you've spoilt it all.'

'I'm sorry.' He stood up distantly. 'I am sorry to have this effect on you. I will leave you before I distress you any more.'

'You're not sorry at all! You do it on purpose, just so that I won't forget my place.'

'And just what do you think your place is?'

'You already know my views on that.'

'You are my wife! Do not forget it!'

'Don't talk to me like that! I don't have to take it from you or anyone else.'

'You are becoming over-excited, Templar,' he snapped. 'As I had expected, my coming here has upset you. You must try and calm yourself.'

'I'm not a child, Leon, so don't treat me as one. But I do think you should go. I'm glad you came to visit me and I thank you for helping me when I fell over, but I'm tired now. I'm afraid I'm not as recovered as I thought I was.'

He gave a slight inclination of his arrogant head. 'Very well. But if you desire me to visit you again perhaps it would be as well if you told Lucy to inform me. I would not like to visit you against your wishes.'

Templar remained stubbornly silent and after a thoughtful look in her direction Leon quietly left the room. Oh, how could he! He knew very well she wouldn't ask Lucy to tell him she wanted him to visit her. It would be too humiliating and he knew it. He knew it! Ooh, she could throw something!

When the doctor next came he agreed that she could start to get up now, but only in short stages. As soon as she tired she was to get straight back into bed. 'Flu wasn't something to be taken lightly as most people did, he reminded her darkly.

'My wife is very stubborn, I'm afraid,' commented Leon.

'Mm,' the doctor frowned deeply. 'In that case it would perhaps be better if Mrs Marcose were carried downstairs and rested there every day. Company will aid her recovery.'

'Then of course she must be taken downstairs,' agreed Leon.

Templar sat in frustrated silence as the two of them discussed her. It was intolerable of them to talk about her like this, as if she couldn't speak for herself.

True to his word Leon carried her effortlessly downstairs later in the afternoon. 'Thank you,' she smiled at him gratefully.

He raised haughty eyebrows at her softening of mood, picking up his jacket from a chair and shrugging his broad shoulders into the fine material. 'I will be home in time to take you back upstairs,' he said distantly.

'You're going out?' She hoped her disappointment wasn't too obvious to him.

'Obviously.'

'But where?'

'Do you think you have the right to question my movements?' he queried mildly, unknowingly very attractive in his dark trousers and the fine linen jacket that accentuated his darkness.

Templar's mouth tightened. 'Don't I?'

'Perhaps,' he admitted slowly. 'Perhaps if you did not behave like a shrew every time I talk to you.'

Her mouth trembled tearfully. 'I don't mean to,' she stumbled over the words.

'Then you should not do it,' Leon said unmercilessly. 'I have tried to be kind to you since we have married, and at times I have thought I was making progress. But it appears we know each other no better than when we first married. If you miss the life you led before we met then I am sorry. But I cannot provide the physical part of our marriage that you obviously crave, and I do not recommend that you find someone else to do so. I will not tolerate any scandal attached to Keri's childhood.'

'What life are you saying I—I led?' she stuttered.

'Your different escorts and your relationships with them. I realise that once you have had those sort of—friendships it is difficult to no longer be able to do so.'

'I—I think you're being insulting, Leon!'

'I think perhaps I am too. But I cannot help it. I find it almost impossible to relate your past life with the girl I am now married to. As Keri's mother you are totally devoted, and yet you were not even sure who her father was,' he shook his head.

'But that wasn't——' Templar broke off. How could she possibly say it wasn't her fault!

'Was not what?' he queried.

'It isn't important. And I'm glad that I now know your opinion of me.'

'Did you ever doubt it?'

'No, I suppose not, although I mistakenly thought you were beginning to like me for myself.' She gave a harsh laugh. 'Silly, wasn't I?'

'Not silly at all. I have tried to treat you with the respect that Keri's mother deserves, in fact I have more than tried, and I believe at times I have succeeded. But the fact that I know your past precludes any closer friendship between the two of us. I cannot accept what your past life has been, and I have no intention of doing so.'

Templar's eyes darkened and she lowered her lids so that he shouldn't see the pain he was inflicting, either intentionally or unintentionally. 'You hate me, don't you?' she asked brokenly.

'I could never hate Keri's mother.'

'Perhaps not, but you hate *me* as a person.'

Leon's eyes narrowed angrily and stepping forward he took her narrow shoulders savagely in his hands and shook her roughly. 'I cannot hate *you* either,' he ground out harshly. 'I wish to God I did!'

Templar stared dazedly up into his dark saturnine face, mesmerised by the harsh handsomeness of his finely etched features. His flinty gaze passed slowly over her big green eyes, over her tiny nose, and lingered caressingly on her slightly parted mouth. His eyes became startlingly blue and Templar gasped at the desire she saw in their depths. 'Leon, I——'

'Silence!' he snapped. 'Be still!'

She was aware of the tight control he had over his feelings and she stared at him in fascination. She had hardly ever seen him lose his cool calmness, and to realise that she was the reason for it was faintly exhilarating.

His fierce gaze was rapier-sharp and his hands tightened momentarily before he roughly pushed her away from him. 'Do you do it on purpose?' he demanded grimly.

'D—do what?'

'Do not be so innocent!' Leon said with disgust. 'You have been nothing but provocative since the first time we met, even going so far as to invade the privacy of my bedroom on one occasion.'

'For no other reason than to tell you your behaviour disgusted me!' Templar retorted hotly.

'No more than yours does me, believe me,' he bit out coldly. 'Perhaps now we have both made our opinions of each other perfectly clear you will learn to leave the subject alone. And me also.'

Templar gasped. 'Why, you—you—I wouldn't touch you if you were the last man on earth!'

'Good,' her husband said with finality. 'For once we are agreed. Goodbye!' The door slammed heavily behind him.

For long seconds Templar continued to stare at that closed door, then turning her body into the chair she began to shake with suppressed tears, allowing her unhappiness free rein.

CHAPTER FIVE

TEMPLAR heaved a shuddering sigh, her face pale and drawn. Keri was fast asleep on her lap and seemed quite unconcerned by the time they had just spent in the air. Templar, always a bad traveller, had been a mass of nerves ever since they had set out for the airport this morning. She had felt even worse when she had realised Leon was to pilot the twelve-seater jet himself. Her eyes had widened with fear and apprehension and she had hesitated nervously about boarding the plane.

Leon had smiled at her mockingly. 'Come, Templar, I do not intend to toss you out over the ocean, convenient though that action may appear.'

Still she hung back, clinging desperately to the unconcerned Keri as she gurgled merrily to herself. 'But I—You don't really intend to fly this machine, do you, Leon? I mean, surely the airport officials wouldn't let you?'

He raised a haughty eyebrow. 'They can hardly prevent me from flying out my own property. Unless of course I am not qualified to do so, but I am, you see.'

His own plane! She ought to have guessed. And that he was a qualified pilot. Such a competent, self-confident man as he was would not let a little thing like obtaining a pilot's licence baulk him in attaining the experience and thrill of piloting himself wherever he wished to go.

'I see,' she licked her suddenly dry lips. 'Do we have to go on this holiday, Leon?' she begged.

His answer was to take her elbow in his firm grasp

and forcefully take her into the luxury of the shiny silver plane's interior. 'Surely you are not admitting your fear to me, Templar? You who have always faced me so bravely and defiantly, no matter what I have accused you of, are surely not afraid of flying? Or is it the pilot that frightens you?'

'I—I've never liked flying.'

'So I do not frighten you?' he persisted.

'No, I have every confidence in you.' She placed Keri in the special cot provided for her. 'I always have.'

Leon looked at her strangely but had not made any reply. He had then left her to enter the cockpit, laughing companionably with the man who was to be the co-pilot.

Templar had sat petrified throughout the whole of the flight, although they had hardly been in the air for any length of time, and Lucy had chattered to her in an attempt to divert her attention from her fear. The younger girl had turned out to be very understanding and although Templar could tell she loved her little charge she always managed to remember that Templar was the child's mother and so had the first claim to her attentions.

Templar's return to comparative good health had taken quite a long time and it was now nearly a month since she had first become ill. True to his word, Leon had carried her downstairs each day, but he had left her immediately on doing so, only returning to assist her back up the stairs. Templar felt that instead of at least getting to know each other in their marriage they were becoming further apart.

Leon came through from the cockpit, a smile of satisfaction on his harsh features. 'And how is my little family?' He looked at her searchingly. 'Are you all right, Templar?'

She laughed brokenly. 'I'll be fine once I get out in the fresh air.' She looked down as Keri began struggling awake in her arms, her face tearful.

'Here,' Leon took the baby into his arms. 'You are not going to cry, are you, little one?' he crooned softly, and miraculously she didn't. Her flushed little face broke into a becoming smile, showing clearly her four white milk-teeth in the front of her mouth. 'That is better,' he chuckled at her self-satisfied expression. 'And now we have to get your mama out into the sunshine and soon she will forget this part of her holiday and look forward to the rest of it, will you not?'

Templar blushed in confusion, her thoughts far away as she watched the two of them together. 'I—I—well, I hope so.'

'You will,' he promised her.

As usual he was proved correct. She soon became enthralled with her new surroundings. A white limousine was waiting for them at the airport, and from the preferential treatment they were all given Templar could only assume Leon often visited here and was well known. He pointed out different places of interest on their drive along the coast, talking quite impersonally of other trips he had made to the villa.

Templar loved the villa on sight, loving its one-floor ranch-like design. It was long and rambling, with possibly half a dozen bedrooms or more, a huge lounge, two large bathrooms and a kitchen which Leon informed her was to remain solely Marie Duval's domain.

'We do not want a strike on our hands,' he told her.

As Templar had no intention of interfering she felt his warning was quite unnecessary. It appeared that the Duvals had their own living accommodation at the side of the villa. Templar had expected the villa to be much smaller than this and so instead of finding a cosy intimate atmosphere she was confronted with the same strangeness of their house in England. Just what had she been expecting, that this would be a normal happy family holiday like other people shared? If she had expected that she was to be sadly disappointed.

Leon handed the sleepy baby over to Lucy. 'Marie will show you to the nursery while I give Mrs Marcose a cup of Marie's excellent coffee. Join us when you are ready, Lucy.'

'Yes, sir.'

Templar accepted the cup of steaming coffee, finding it just as delicious as he had said it would be. 'What do you plan to do with the rest of the day?' she asked conversationally.

He shrugged his broad shoulders. 'What do most people do on holiday? I intend to have a leisurely lunch and then spend the afternoon soaking up the sun on the glorious beach at the back of the villa.'

Her eyes opened wide, showing her surprise. 'You do? But don't you have any work you should be doing?'

'Should I have?'

She shrugged. 'But I thought this would be a business trip for you.'

'Then you thought wrong. This will suffice as the honeymoon most people think we have anticipated.' He saw her shocked look. 'It is true. My friends have all accepted Keri as my child, and they all know that we have only been married a matter of weeks rather than years.'

'Are they shocked?'

'Why should they be shocked? I am a man and you are very much a woman.'

'I'd be shocked in the same circumstances.'

'You do not preach what you practise,' was his parting comment.

Templar was more formally introduced to the French couple who looked after the villa at lunchtime, and found that although they understood English they spoke the language very little themselves. Marie seemed to be smiling most of the time and Templar thought she was going to prove very pleasant. Keri was an instant hit with both the Duvals.

She looked at Leon as her attention was caught and held by the mention of Alex, Leon's brother. 'What did she say?' she whispered once Marie had bustled away. 'About Alex, I mean.'

Leon shrugged. 'It was not important.'

'But you look—annoyed.'

He stood up, taking his freshly poured coffee with him. 'I am not annoyed. Marie merely said that now I have Keri perhaps it will help me over Alex's death.' He stared sightlessly at the beautiful golden beach before him.

'I see,' she bit her lip nervously.

Leon turned sharply to face her. 'And just what do you see, Templar? I wish I could understand you, get behind that exterior of yours. Does the fact that your child's father is dead not worry you at all? Or did you just not care enough?'

'I've told you——'

'Told me what?' His eyes narrowed to grey slits. 'You have told me nothing. When I ask if you loved Alex, you say that Keri was born out of love, *not* that you loved my brother, but that *Keri* was born out of love. You are evasive and you prevaricate. I ask what this girl Tiffany means to you and you say she was a friend. Does the death of a friend a year ago affect you more than the death of the man you were supposed to love? Does it?'

'Tiffany was—she was a very close friend.' Templar

was pale, she couldn't meet the fierceness of his gaze. 'Closer than Alex?'

'Alex and—and I had parted company before I even knew about Keri. Tiffany was a lifelong friend.' She still kept her head lowered.

'And Alex was your lover!'

Templar hung her head. She had no way of getting herself out of this situation other than blatantly lying, something she had so far managed not to do. 'Alex was —He didn't love me!'

'I know that!' Leon snapped. 'Alex loved a girl called Tiffany—a girl that you appear to know too. Did you know he loved this other girl?'

She stared at him in wonder. 'How do you know Alex loved Tiffany?'

'Because he chose to tell me so! Did you know about it?' he repeated.

Templar shook her head dazedly. Alex had loved Tiffany! It seemed too good to be true. 'I—No—no, I didn't know. I knew Tiffany loved him, but not until— not until she died.'

'Perhaps she was afraid to tell you, this friend of yours? Perhaps she was afraid that your jealousy would lead you to do something stupid, something that would take Alex away from her, perhaps inform him of your condition and so make him honour bound to marry you, as I have done. I take it your friend knew of the coming baby?' His eyes were rapier-sharp.

She could almost have laughed at such a question if she wasn't feeling quite so inwardly elated at the shared love of Keri's parents. And yet there were still questions unanswered, questions that might never be answered now. Such as, if Alex had loved Tiffany why had he spurned her when she was to have had his child, and why two people so much in love had died not knowing of that love. So many questions, and no one alive to answer them.

She couldn't look at her husband, hating more and more the contempt she never failed to see in his eyes for her even when he wasn't being taunting. 'Yes, she knew,' she told him bluntly.

'I thought as much. So she made no effort to contact my brother because she knew you were to have his child?'

'No, she didn't, she——' She broke off in confusion, realising she had almost said too much to this very shrewd man who was her husband.

'Yes? She—what?'

Templar shook her head. 'Nothing. It isn't important.'

Leon strode angrily across the room to stare furiously down at her. 'It may not be important to you, but it matters very much to me!'

'Why?' she asked sneeringly, attack the best form of defence. 'So that you can at last be convinced that your brother never erred enough to love someone as worthless as me? What do you want to know, Leon? That your brother loved Tiffany as she loved him, that she was good and kind and gentle and everything I'm not? Well, she was all of those things, every single one.' Her voice broke emotionally. 'And I loved her very much.'

'Enough to take Alex away from her? Or did you just share him without this paragon of a Tiffany's knowledge?' His mouth turned back in a sneer. 'That is the answer, is it not? You and Alex were meeting each other secretly.'

'We were not!' She shook her head. 'I don't have to answer any more of these questions. Leave me alone, Leon. Just leave me alone!'

He forced her chin round roughly so that she faced

him. 'No, I will not! This time there will be no escape for you. You will tell me of your relationship with Alex. All of it. And also what you know about this Tiffany that he loved. I never met her, I would be interested to hear about her.'

Templar swallowed hard. 'I—She——'

'Come, Templar,' he said cruelly. 'Do not pretend hurt with me. I know you, remember? I know that you were not even sure of your own child's parentage, that you allowed your employer liberties not usual in such a relationship. And he was a married man too! Oh yes, I saw his wedding ring. Do you make a habit of stealing other women's men? Does it add to the excitement?'

'Would you like me to say yes?'

'I would like you to tell me the truth!'

Templar stood up, glaring at him angrily. 'Then the answer is yes! I'm all the things you think I am. *Now* will you leave me alone? Before I married you things were hard moneywise, but I certainly never had to put up with the verbal abuse you dish out. I was quite well off really,' she laughed brokenly. 'If only I'd known what it was going to be like! I would never have sent that letter if I'd known Alex was dead. I would rather have starved than be married to a despot. But I wasn't given the choice, was I? Oh no, the mighty Marcose had to have it all his own way. Well, you have it all, Leon, a beautiful daughter and a shrewish wife. Does it please you?'

'You are lying to me, Templar. You want me to think badly of you. Why? What do you hope to achieve by it?'

'Freedom?'

'Freedom to do what? Live without seeing your child grow up to be as beautiful as her mother?' He shook his head. 'You could not do it.'

'No, and you know it. That's why you say these horrible things to me, why you ignore me whenever possible. It's because you know I can't hit back as I would like to do. You know I couldn't leave Keri, you've always known it. If I cared for her less I wouldn't be married to you and tormented at every turn.'

'*You* are tormented,' Leon said tersely. 'How do you think I feel, married to a woman it is impossible to get close to?'

Templar's green eyes widened. 'But you said—you said our marriage wasn't to be—to be——'

'It is not! But it would be more comfortable for both of us if we could become friends.'

'Do you honestly think we could?' she asked in disbelief. 'After all that's been said and done?'

Leon shrugged. 'We could try. It would perhaps help if you would tell me about this Tiffany. How did you know her?'

'She was a model too. We were friends. And she loved Alex, I know that. What I don't understand is why, if they loved each other, they were forced apart. And it wasn't through anything said or done on my part. I was out of the country at the time.'

'I know that, not that you were out of the country, but that you did not break them up. I was responsible for that. Alex was already betrothed.'

'But they were in love, Leon!'

His face was a tormented mask. 'I thought it was a fleeting thing, that these feelings of love Alex professed to have for this girl would soon pass.'

'So what did you do?' she asked softly, aware that he wanted to talk, to tell her of his brother as he had probably told no one else.

Leon ran a hand through his thick vibrant hair. 'I

asked Alex not to see this girl for three months, not to even get in touch with her, and see how he felt then.'

'And how did he feel?'

'He loved her still,' he said resignedly. 'I am sorry, this must be painful for you too. But Alex loved this Tiffany still. I had made him write her a letter saying he would see her no more. I told him that if they truly loved each other they would be together again after the three months.'

'So you were testing Tiffany, seeing how she would react to such a letter?'

'Yes! But I paid for it, I paid for it dearly.'

And so had Tiffany, her baby making it impossible for her to go to her lover. She would never have known if he wanted her or just felt responsible for the baby. 'What happened, Leon?' she asked.

He was grey now, as if talking about it brought him pain. But she knew he wanted to talk. 'Alex waited the three months and at the end of that time, with my permission, he went to see her.'

'But he—he didn't,' Templar shook her head. 'I was with her when she died and she hadn't seen him for months, not since that letter.'

'She loved him still?'

'Very much.'

He took a deep ragged breath. 'Alex was killed on his way to see her,' he explained simply. 'So it was my fault, all of it. They would perhaps have been happy now, and instead they are both dead.'

Templar took a step towards him, hesitant about comforting him in case he rejected her. 'You can't blame yourself, Leon. Tiffany would have died anyway. I spoke to the doctor, so I know.'

'It might not have happened if she had had Alex with her. But I also lost my brother, that is why

Keri means so much to me—she is all I have left of him.'

To Templar it seemed they had dwelt enough on the past. 'Let's go out on to the beach, Leon,' she suggested gently. 'You came away to relax, not blame yourself for something that happened in the past, something that is over and can never be changed. I can assure you that nothing could have been done for Tiffany, the doctor assured me that there was no hope. We'll go down to the beach now and begin our holiday.'

He looked unapproachable. 'You might be able to forget it as easily as that, but I certainly cannot. My brother might still be alive if I had not——'

'Stop it, Leon! Don't torture yourself any more. Neither would have been happy without the other. You have Keri's future to think of now, not dwell on the past.'

Leon nodded, some of the rigidity starting to leave his features. 'You are right. But I also have your future to think about too.'

She smiled at him gently, more touched than she cared to admit that he had confided his feelings of guilt to her. But she meant what she had said, they must think of the future now, not think of the past. In a way they were both to blame for what had happened, she for leaving Tiffany alone in England when she could perhaps have helped Leon to understand this young couple's love for each other, and Leon for rejecting their emotions out of hand. Perhaps she, Templar, should feel hate towards this man for causing Tiffany all that misery, but somehow she couldn't do so. At the time he had felt he was doing the right thing for everyone, he had no way of knowing its outcome.

'If that's so then we can easily settle my immediate future. I'd like to go swimming please.'

He shook his head, smiling dazedly. 'You are very persistent, are you not?'

'Very,' she agreed.

'Then come, we will collect our beach things and do as you suggest. Keri will be perfectly all right with Lucy,' he answered her question before she even asked it. 'You must learn to designate some of her care to Lucy while we are here. After all, you are here to rest.'

Templar laughed, feeling more at ease with him now than she ever had before. Perhaps this holiday was going to be a success after all. She followed him up to their adjoining bedrooms. 'I feel such a fraud,' she laughed. 'Here to rest! Why, I haven't worked in two months.'

'You worked long and hard before that,' he spoke to her through the open connecting door as they gathered together their swimming clothes. 'Tell me, do you miss your life as a model?'

She stared thoughtfully into the mirror in front of her, noting the still smooth complexion, clear green eyes and long shining hair. She was still as beautiful as she ever had been, and yet there was no longer that drive within her, the need to get to the top. All ambition had left her, and in its place she had the contentment of caring for the baby. She shook her head firmly. 'Not at all. Why?' she teased. 'Are you considering sending me out to work?'

'Certainly not! The Marcose women do not work.'

She stood in the open doorway, watching his unhurried movements. 'So I'm a Marcose woman now, am I?' she asked with amusement.

'But of course,' Leon replied arrogantly. 'You are my wife. Now,' he quirked a mocking eyebrow, 'unless you wish to watch me undress, I suggest you go to your own bathroom and change.'

'Oh—oh, yes!' Her face suffused with colour as she made her way hastily to the bathroom, followed by Leon's throaty chuckle.

Her bikini was a new acquisition, bought for her by Leon on a shopping spree shortly before the holiday. There was a matching green beachrobe, and both matched her eyes perfectly, also bringing out the red colour of her long hair. She donned the beachrobe before meeting Leon, feeling almost naked in the scantiness of the minute bikini. She only hoped it would stand the test of actually being in water, so many of them didn't nowadays.

Leon felt none of her shyness, dressed only in royal blue bathing trunks. And looking breathtakingly attractive! Tall and lithe, his body was pure ripcord muscle, tanned, his stomach muscles flat and firm, his shoulders broad and powerful. The hair on his chest was thick and dark, a gold medallion secured about his neck with a thick chunky gold chain. They walked down to the beach in companionable silence, Templar glancing occasionally at the engraving on the medallion, sure that she had seen the markings before.

'Of course!' she burst out excitely. 'My ring!'

He looked at her closely. 'You have lost it?' He frowned, lifting up her left hand and touching the wide gold band that adorned her finger. 'But no, you still have it. You are talking of another ring, perhaps?'

She laughed. 'No. Your medallion and my ring, they have the same engraving.'

The frown disappeared from his brow. 'It is the family emblem,' he explained.

'A bird of prey,' she said softly, looking at the soaring eagle engraved on both pieces of jewellery.

'Yes,' he grinned, flashing white teeth in his deeply tanned face. 'Apt, would you not say?'

'Maybe,' she agreed, smiling. She undid her beach-robe and threw it down on to the sand before running to the shoreline, self-conscious in the bikini's revealing design. 'Race you!' she challenged.

He raised an eyebrow. 'And what is the prize to be?'

She blushed at the deep look in his eyes. 'Whatever you want it to be,' she answered daringly.

'In that case I accept the challenge.' He threw down his towel and joined her, running appreciative eyes over her slender body, from her long slender legs, over her narrow hips, flat stomach, and full breasts.

'And the prize?' She waited for his answer, excitement in her look.

Leon's eyes darkened. 'Whoever loses must rub suntan oil on the other's back,' he said mockingly.

'Oh.' She did her best to hide her disappointment, sure that he had been going to say something different. 'I might just lose on purpose,' she replied brightly. 'I like oil rubbed on my back.'

Leon laughed, a completely natural laugh. 'So do I, so it would appear it is to be a race to lose.'

He won, as she had known he would; swimming wasn't one of her better activities. But she enjoyed rubbing the oil on his back anyway. His skin felt firm and smooth, and she loved the feel of it. Leon lay perfectly still under her ministrations, the smile on his face evidence of his enjoyment.

'Mmm,' he rolled over on to his back. 'You are quite good, you must have done this before.'

'No, I—You're teasing me, Leon!' she admonished.

'I am amazed at your capacity for blushing. I thought you a woman of the world.'

That brought her up with a start. 'Excuse me,' she said sarcastically. 'I'd forgotten my role in life for a moment. It won't happen again.'

Leon lay on his stomach, staring out to sea, his hair dried by the sun. 'Again you are on the defensive. I was merely making an unbiased observation.'

'Sorry.' She lay down a small distance away from him, her sunglasses pushed over her nose, her eyes closed.

Her eyes flew open again as she felt a drop of water fall on her arm. Leaning above her, his face only inches away from her own, Leon looked darkly down at her. Her heart began to beat erratically at his closeness, her breath suddenly constricted.

'You are not sorry at all,' he said huskily. 'You deliberately bait me until I have to retaliate.'

'W—what do you mean?' she asked breathlessly.

His hand gently removed a strand of hair from her face, smoothing one creamy cheek. 'You force me to do these things, Templar,' he groaned. 'I have vowed to myself that I would not touch you, but lately I have found myself—' He swung away from her, staring bleakly out to sea again. 'This is madness!'

Templar put out a hand and tentatively touched his bare shoulder. 'What is, Leon?' She knew she was playing with fire, but something pushed her on, forcing her to reach out to him, to touch him somehow.

He pushed her hand away angrily. 'Leave me alone, Templar! Do you not know when to leave well alone?'

'But I——'

He rolled back towards her, imprisoning her between his arms. He looked down at her, putting out one of his hands and running it caressingly over the smooth contours of her waist and hips. 'So soft,' he murmured as if to himself. 'Beautiful and soft.'

Templar remained silent and still. His touch wasn't unpleasant, in fact it was rather stimulating. Apart from Ken, Leon was the only man she had been this close to in a year, although this was far from the only reason his touch affected her. In all her travels, abroad and in England, she had never met a man as fascinating and attractive as Leon.

When she had first met him she had thought him arrogant and stern, but she had learnt during the last weeks that his chilly exterior shielded a man who lived and worked alone, who pushed all personal things out of his life. But he could no longer do that, he now had a wife and child to think of, and those barriers he had erected about his emotions were slowly crumbling.

'Leon . . .' she said throatily.

He seemed not to have heard her, looking down at her body as if fascinated. 'Your figure is—perfect. Who would ever think you had had a baby just twelve short months ago?'

But she hadn't. She hadn't! Her deception entered into their every conversation. 'Leon, I——'

'Do not interrupt, Templar,' he told her deeply, slowly bending his head to caress her throat with his firm lips.

Her pulse quickened and her skin burnt where he touched. She had never thought of herself as a physical person, and yet Leon's slightest touch was sending her into nerve-shattering ecstasy. She fought for control of her senses, but she could no longer think straight. His lips and hands were doing strange things to her body and her arms moved up to encircle his neck of their own volition.

'Oh, Leon!' she sighed throatily.

'Do you like my hands upon your body?' he groaned, his eyes a sleepy blue with his passion.

'I——'

'Do not answer!' he snapped tautly, rolling away from her in self-disgust. 'I had no right to ask you that, no right to touch you at all!' He pushed his hair away from his forehead. 'I am returning to the villa now, you must return when you are ready.'

'But, Leon!' she cried desperately, sitting up in the sand as he gathered up his towel in preparation for leaving. 'Do you have to go?' she asked softly.

He looked down at her with tormented eyes. 'I have to go.'

Templar didn't see him leave, but nevertheless she knew he had gone, she could no longer sense his presence. Leon was becoming important to her—and she didn't like it! She and Tiffany had only ever relied on each other, but it seemed that both of them were to find the Marcoses the men they would rely on. But she didn't *want* to rely on him! Already she was beginning to depend on him too much, become too involved with their little family unit.

What would a child of Leon's look like? Probably very like Keri, she thought dreamily. And it would look like her too, so much so that she felt sure no one would ever be able to tell the two children weren't actually brother and sister.

She brought her thoughts up with a start. Whatever was she thinking of! There could never be a child between Leon and herself. Never! Even if they became close enough for such a relationship to be possible, which she seriously doubted, she could not allow it to happen. Once Leon tried to go any further than a few kisses he would know she was completely inexperienced, and he would certainly know she had never borne a child. And he would never forgive her for lying about Keri's parentage. He wasn't a forgiving man.

But could they live the rest of their lives without human warmth? She doubted it. Leon was a virile man, and she didn't like the thought of him making love to another woman, someone like Rachel for instance. No, she didn't like that idea at all.

Leon avoided any personal subjects throughout dinner, both of them ever conscious of Marie as she waited on them. But once dinner was over it was a different matter, Leon requesting that she join him in the privacy of the lounge for coffee. She poured him the desired black coffee, sipping nervously at her own milky brew.

He seemed in no hurry to speak and as each moment slowly ticked by Templar became more and more agitated. Finally she sighed deeply. 'For goodness' sake, Leon! Just say whatever it was you wanted to say and get it over with.'

His eyes were chillingly grey as he looked down at her from his great height as she sat in one of the white leather armchairs. 'I have, of course, to apologise for what happened this afternoon. It was not my intention to touch you.'

Templar blushed. 'I—Please! It wasn't important.'

'But it was,' he said firmly. 'My actions were not the ones you expected of me, the man who promised you a completely uninvolved marriage.'

'By uninvolved, you mean . . .?'

'I mean, no *physical* involvement. You have stood enough in your young life already without being forced into a physical relationship you would find repellent.'

'Oh, but I——'

'Please, Templar, let me finish! I wish you to forget what took place between us on the beach, try to put it out of your mind.'

She shook her head. 'I couldn't forget it, Leon. Surely you realise it must change things between us?'

Leon moved to the drinks tray, helping himself to a

liberal amount of whisky before answering her. 'That I momentarily forgot our true state and found myself desiring you cannot be changed, but it must be forgotten. And it will not be repeated,' he added sternly.

'How can you be so sure?' she persisted perversely, perversely because she herself found this subject highly embarrassing. But she couldn't let the subject drop, forcing him to answer her. 'Leon?'

He slammed the glass down on the table. 'Because I will not allow it to happen again! I am not an impressionable schoolboy who can be aroused at the merest touch of a beautiful woman. I do have some control, even though you may doubt it.'

'And what about me?'

He looked surprised. 'What about you?'

'I wasn't—well, I——'. She stumbled over the words.

His face became set. 'You were not unmoved?' he finished coldly. 'But I know that, I am not a fool. It was to be expected that you would eventually turn to me for what physical comfort you could find. A woman is much like a man in that respect. The human body, once it has known such pleasures, demands more. And I——'

'Yes?' she asked shrilly. 'You *what*?' Her eyes sparkled dangerously as she stood up to face him. 'I've never heard such a lot of rubbish in my life! You talk about making love as if it's a clinical thing, not something that happens impulsively, with breathtaking feeling and love. Yes, I was aroused by your touch, but I certainly wouldn't have let you make love to me. My body demands nothing, nothing at all!'

She spoke the words with feeling, but she wasn't sure she meant them. When he had left her this afternoon she had felt bereft, as if she had been on the verge of a great discovery but had then been denied that knowledge.

'You are upset,' Leon said calmly. 'And you are saying things that if you thought about them, you would know for yourself to be untrue. It is a problem I have no answer to. I will not permit you to take a lover, that I just cannot allow.'

Templar gave a choking laugh. 'Oh, God,' she choked. 'I don't believe this is happening! I don't want a lover, Leon! I just want to be left alone to live my life and bring up my daughter. It was you who introduced the subject of physical gratification—I had no thoughts on the subject.'

'Do not delude yourself, Templar,' he scoffed. 'I have seen the way you look at me when you think I am not looking. I have seen the look of curiosity enter your eyes. Like all women, you begin to wonder what it would be like to be made love to by that man or this, and your attention has now come around to me. You are curious as to what makes me tick, are you not?'

She was furious now. 'I know what makes you tick! That computer you have inside you for a heart. Do you have to analyse everything? Does nothing you do ever happen spontaneously?'

'Sometimes. I am a man,' he answered simply. 'And men are prone to give in to the senses rather than the mind.'

'Not you, Leon,' she said fiercely. 'You weigh everything up before coming to a decision, work everything out coldly until it meets your approval, and then carry it out.'

'My actions this afternoon were neither clinical nor thought out.' He looked at her coldly.

'No,' she admitted. 'Which means there may be hope for you yet.'

'There will be no more lapses of that kind,' he told her haughtily.

'We'll see, Leon,' she said softly. 'We'll see.'

CHAPTER SIX

TEMPLAR found her feelings towards Leon changing over the next few days. No longer did she think of him as the cold arrogant man of their first meeting, but as a sensually alive man who could be moved to passion like any other. And she had evoked those feelings, no matter how much he tried to deny it. It had been *her*, and not just any woman, that he had reacted to. And she also knew he despised his weakness, fought against it with everything he could.

She found herself looking forward to the long lazy days they spent together on the beach, Keri joining them until it became too hot for her to play in comfort. If occasionally Leon avoided being with Templar he never neglected to spend time with the baby, the two of them having become firm friends, a bond of love existing between them that could never be broken.

On the fourth morning of their stay Templar received a letter from Mary. What she read there made her eyes fill with tears. She looked at Leon, her sudden stillness causing him to put down the newspaper he had been reading with his breakfast and look at her enquiringly.

'Is anything wrong?' He looked pointedly at the letter.

'Why did you do it, Leon?' she asked brokenly.

'Why did I do what?' He frowned his puzzlement.

She held up the letter. 'This is from Mary.'

'Ah!' His brow cleared.

'It was such a kind thing to do, to buy them a house

like that. I can hardly believe it!'

'I have not bought them a house,' he corrected. 'For some reason they insist on paying me back the money. I wanted to make them a gift of the place, God knows I can afford it, but Peter would not hear of it. Not even when I said it was a gift for my godson.'

Templar laughed lightly. 'A house is rather a strange gift for a month-old baby.' She sobered. 'Even for someone as rich as you are. What made you make such a strange gesture?'

He shrugged, folding up the newspaper in readiness for leaving the breakfast-table. 'They are your friends,' he said simply.

Her eyes widened. 'And—and that made you buy them a house?'

'But of course. You were unhappy for your friend, especially now they have Daniel. I merely alleviated that unhappiness. As I have the money it was quite a simple thing to do.'

'But not something many people would have done.'

His eyes became distant. 'Do not make it more important than it is. I have merely loaned them a sum of money, it is a business deal if you like.'

She gave a half-smile. 'With you the loser. Mary says that you insist the money should be interest-free. That doesn't seem a very good business deal to me.'

'I disagree with you. It has made you happy, has it not?'

'Very,' she agreed.

'Then it was worth every penny.' He stood up, cutting short their conversation. But Templar would not be put off so easily.

'Why should you want me to feel happy, Leon? I didn't think that was part of your plans at all.'

'We will not argue, Templar,' he said stiffly.

'That's always your line of defence, isn't it? With-draw from me in your arrogant manner. I can't even have a normal conversation with you!'

He looked down at her haughtily. 'This is not a normal conversation, none of them have been since I made the mistake of kissing you the other day. And it was a mistake, believe me.'

'But you didn't—kiss me, I mean.' She blushed under his scathing look.

'The fact that our lips did not meet does not mean I did not kiss you.' He turned away. 'I am sure you re-member very well what I did.'

'You touched and caressed me! Is that a sin?'

'You ask me that?' he shook his head. 'You have my brother's child,' he said with finality.

Templar rose from the table too, twisting her hands together in her tension. 'And if I didn't, what then? Would you still have this aversion to touching me?'

Leon's eyes became more distant with each word she spoke. 'As the situation does not arise I can really see no——'

'Would you!' she demanded between clenched teeth.

He shook his head. 'I cannot answer that.'

'Why?' Her eyes glinted. 'Because you're afraid to? Because you're frightened of admitting to any of the more basic feelings the rest of us are blessed with? You aren't a machine, Leon, no matter how much you pre-tend to be. So answer the question!'

'Do not take that tone with me!'

'Answer it, Leon!'

The rigidity left his body and he turned away. 'You are like a child who will not be put off. If,' he chose his words carefully, 'If you were not Keri's mother then I admit, reluctantly, that I would find you very desirable.

But you are her mother, so the situation does not arise.'
He walked to the door.

'W—where are you going?' she asked.

'I will be out all day today. I have an appointment.'

'Oh, yes?'

'Yes,' his mouth tightened. 'A business appointment.'

'Have a nice day,' she said flippantly. 'And don't—
don't *work* too hard, will you?'

Leon looked quickly at his watch. 'I do not have the
time to argue with you further. We will have to continue this discussion when I return.'

'Hardly a discussion,' she scoffed. 'It can hardly be
that when you run away from situations all the time.
Oh, go away, Leon,' she dismissed.

'You will push me too far one day, Templar,' he
warned grimly. 'And when that day comes I will not be
responsible for my actions.'

'I can hardly wait,' she returned scathingly.

His answer was to slam the door behind him as he
left. Oh, damn! Templar looked down at her nearly
full breakfast plate, no longer feeling even remotely
hungry. Poor Leon, he couldn't even discuss personal
subjects now without them developing into a full-scale
argument.

The trouble was she was too much aware of him
now, aware of him as a man, as her own husband. He
was a very attractive individual, with that dark over-
long hair touched with grey at the temples, smouldering
sexy eyes that could be icily grey or passionately blue,
firm straight nose and mouth, with that full sensuous
lower lip, and his tall lean attractive body. From the
first moment they had met she had been wholly aware
of him as a dominant personality, but now he was all
male to her, all overwhelmingly male.

She forced a smile on her face as she heard Lucy ap-

proaching with Keri. She and Leon had tried to keep
their antipathy from everyone but themselves, acting
as much like a normal married couple in front of others
as they were able to, although this proved difficult at
times. And this was one of those times.

Lucy came in, all smiles, holding Keri who was
chuckling happily as usual. Dressed in her tiny bathing
costume, plus nappy, and a flowered sun hat, she was
all ready to go down to the beach.

'Hello, darling!' Templar took the willing Keri into
her arms. 'It looks as if we'll have to go down on our
own, poppet, Daddy's gone out today.'

'Oh.' Lucy looked uncertain. 'Would you—would
you like me to come down with you?'

'No. It's your day off. You're going into the village,
aren't you?'

'Just to have a look around,' Lucy shrugged. 'I can
put it off if you would rather I——'

'Certainly not.' Templar chucked Keri under the
chin. 'We can manage on our own for one day, you take
your day off. This is partly your holiday too.'

'Well . . . if you're sure?'

'I'm sure. And thank you for getting Keri ready.'

It was already warm on the beach, and she placed
Keri on the spread blanket before sitting down herself.
It was a beautiful beach, totally private, with none of
the noise and chatter one usually associated with a
holiday beach. But then this was no ordinary holiday
beach, this was owned and used exclusively by Leon's
family or guests.

Templar watched Keri playing for several long
minutes, conscious of how happy and less fretful her
niece had become. Leon had erected a make-do playpen for Keri on the beach and they usually put her in
there while they swam, which she did now. Keri didn't

mind the playpen at all, and as it was over an hour since she had eaten her little piece of breakfast she thought it quite safe for her to swim.

Templar lay on her back lazing in the clear blue water, gazing at the completely cloudless sky above her. She was missing Leon today, strange, but true. They had been together so much the last few days that she had come to expect it, desire his company even. But where was her pride, that stiff-necked independence that had taken her through so much in the past year? It appeared that she was slowly losing the desire to be independent, that she in fact enjoyed relying on Leon. Somehow it had happened without her being aware of it.

Something touched her ankle, breaking her mood and throwing her into a confused panic. She came up spluttering, her hair plastered to her forehead, and glared furiously into a pair of laughing brown eyes. 'Just what do you think you're doing?' she demanded angrily.

The man trod water beside her, grinning widely. 'Until a few seconds ago I was swimming along quite happily, and then this mermaid with glorious red hair wandered into my view. Of course, I had to investigate.'

'Oh, of course. But what do you mean by startling me like that? You frightened the life out of me!' She was still trying to get some of the strands of hair out of her eyes.

He looked at her reproachfully. 'It wasn't exactly my fault. I did speak to you first, but you didn't seem to hear me.'

'Oh.' She grudgingly admitted that he was a nice-looking man, of about thirty. Out of the water he was probably quite tall, at least six foot, she would say. He had the over-long styled hair that was fashionable nowadays, good-looking features, even white teeth, and a tanned muscled body. 'And what are you doing here?'

'Here precisely, or here France?'

'Here precisely,' she smiled reluctantly.

He laughed. 'Would you believe, swimming?'

Templar looked about them impatiently. 'Look, can we go back to the beach? I have a feeling my baby might be getting fretful.'

'Sure.'

Once ashore she towelled her hair dry, offering the stranger her spare towel, which he gratefully accepted. Keri had fallen asleep in the bottom of the playpen and wasn't fretful at all.

'I'm Neil Adams, by the way.' He slumped down on to the golden sand beside her.

'Templar Marcose,' she supplied self-consciously, still not quite sure of her newly acquired surname.

'That's a nice baby you have there.'

'Thank you, I think so too.'

'And so does your husband. I've seen him from a distance playing with her a couple of times.' His eyes narrowed in the glare of the sun.

'My husband?' she questioned sharply. 'When did you see him?'

'The last couple of days. I've seen all three of you together on the beach. Your husband isn't with you today?' He laid the damp towel out in the sun to dry.

She averted her eyes. 'Not today.'

Neil Adams was watching her closely. 'I feel I should know you,' he remarked quizzically. 'And that isn't a line, I genuinely believe I should recognise you.'

Templar knew it wasn't a line because she had had the same feeling about him for the last couple of minutes. Everything about him seemed familiar. 'Do you live in London?' she asked.

He shook his head. 'I live here. But London used to be my home. I have the next villa up the coast to this one, that's why I've seen so much of you.' His brow cleared suddenly. 'Templar!' he burst out. 'Of course, Templar *Newman*! I wondered what had happened to you. I'm a photographer,' he explained, 'and a couple of months ago I decided I wanted you for one of my assignments. I called round all the agencies, but all they could tell me was that you were no longer on their books.'

'I've given up modelling,' she said quietly.

'So I gathered. But isn't it strange that you were just a few minutes away from me all the time?'

'I doubt if I was at the time.' She rubbed oil into her sensitive skin. 'We've only been here a week.' She looked at him sharply. 'When you say Neil Adams, do you mean *the* Neil Adams?'

'Depends what you mean by *the*,' he said bashfully.

'The famous and exclusive photographer.'

'I suppose I could be,' he admitted.

Templar's eyes glowed. 'There's no *suppose* about it, it is you. And you wanted me for some photographs?'

'I still do. Only you have the exact colour hair that I wanted for some sunset pictures I intend taking. I don't suppose you would consider coming out of retirement for a few days?'

She shook her head, well aware of Leon's opinion on that. 'I'm afraid not. But there must be plenty of models about with my colour hair, I can't believe it's unique.'

'It isn't, if I wanted it out of a bottle. I don't. I would stake my reputation on your hair being natural.'

'It is,' she admitted blushingly.

'It's a damned shame you're out of circulation, you're just what I wanted.' He looked disappointed.

'Well, I can't say I'm not flattered. I mean, you're Neil Adams! It would have been the height of my career to be photographed by you.' Templar couldn't hide her disappointment. Once photographed by this man she would have been made careerwise.

'Wouldn't your husband let you do just this one assignment? If I can't use you I'm going to scrap the idea.' He sat up, watching her closely.

Templar looked regretful. 'Leon doesn't approve of working wives.'

Neil frowned. 'Leon? You're married to Leon Marcose?'

'Do you know him?'

He shrugged. 'Not exactly know him, we've met a couple of times, that's all. I knew his brother better.'

'Alex?' she asked sharply, still much too sensitive where Keri's father was concerned. 'You knew Alex?'

'Mm,' he narrowed his eyes as he looked out to sea. 'I was sorry to hear of his death. I should think Leon was devastated, they were very close.'

'Yes,' she agreed quietly.

Neil turned to smile gently at her. 'At least he had you to help him through it all. There's nothing worse than being on your own when something like that happens.'

'Oh, I wasn't married to Leon at the time,' she answered without thinking.

She inwardly cringed as she saw him look from year-old Keri and back to herself, making a quick calculation and coming to the wrong conclusion. 'I see.' He looked embarrassed. 'Well, at least he has you now.'

'It isn't what you think, you know,' she began. 'I wish I could explain, but——'

'You don't have to explain anything to me. Why should I care when the two of you got married, it's none of my business. Are you here on holiday?' he changed the subject.

'For a couple of weeks, although it seems that Leon also has some business to take care of too.' And after saying he wouldn't be working!

Neil stood up. 'I must say I didn't even recognise him, but then I only saw him from out there,' he indicated the sea. 'Perhaps I can see you tomorrow? I have to get back to the villa right now, I have guests staying. Is it all right if I drop over tomorrow?'

She looked up at him. 'I suppose so, but I——' she hesitated about explaining her uncertainty.

He grinned down at her. 'Don't worry, Templar. I know I've only met Leon a couple of times, but I think it was enough to tell me what sort of a husband he would make. And looking at you I wouldn't blame him.'

'Thank you. And thank you for understanding. It's just that Leon wouldn't like to think of me meeting you like this. He's very possessive.' Suspicious was the word she would have liked to have used. Leon was suspicious of her every move.

'Right. Maybe I'll see you tomorrow, then.'

'That would be lovely.' She watched regretfully as he entered the sea again and set out towards his home with firm even strokes.

She wasn't given much time to dwell on her new acquaintance or think what it would have meant for her to be photographed by the famous Neil Adams, for at that moment Keri woke up and made it impossible for her to think of anything but her. She soon stopped crying, but after that decided she wanted to paddle in the shallow water.

Consequently Templar didn't even get a moment to herself until she was changing for dinner. Keri was fast asleep in the room that had been converted into a nursery for her, after an uproarious bathtime, and Lucy was keeping an ear cocked in case she stirred, not that she very often did nowadays. As far as Templar was aware Leon hadn't yet returned from his business meeting, but she changed for dinner anyway.

She had finished dinner and was having coffee in the lounge when he returned. She made an effort to look cool, although she had been quite worried about him. She watched below lowered lids as he poured himself a whisky and came to stand in front of the sofa she was sitting on.

'Good evening,' came his stiff greeting.

'I've already eaten,' she replied coolly, ignoring the social pleasantries.

'So have I, I ate in town.' He sipped his whisky.

'Really? Didn't it occur to you to let me know? I had no idea you didn't intend returning for dinner.'

'Neither did I. The—business meeting went on for longer than I intended.'

Her look sharpened at his hesitation. 'Really?'

His glass landed on the coffee-table with a crash and she was surprised it showed no signs of breakage. She looked up to meet the angry glitter of steely grey eyes. 'What are you implying now? That I have not been to a business meeting? That I have perhaps been seeing another woman?'

Templar was taken aback by his attack. He was certainly angry, but he looked very attractive in his anger. He wasn't dressed for a business meeting, the dazzling white shirt and trousers emphasising the darkness of his skin, his hair brushed back casually so that a few strands lay over his forehead. His lips were pressed together angrily and there were fine lines either side of that firm mouth and nose, his grey-blue eyes narrowed furiously.

'Well, I——' she began uncertainly.

He picked up the glass and drank the remaining whisky in one gulp. 'You sound like a jealous wife—*my* wife!'

She stood up, as angry as he now. 'I'm not jealous, Leon. I wasn't anything until you came in. What on earth's the matter with you that you come home in this mood?'

'There is nothing wrong with me that a little less suspicion on your part would not cure.'

'I wasn't suspicious!' She felt like stamping her foot childishly in anger. 'But I am now,' she amended. 'Why are you on the defensive?'

'I am not!' He marched purposefully towards the door. 'I am going to my bedroom.'

'But, Leon, it's only early yet. And I haven't seen you all day,' she pouted sulkily.

'I have some business papers to sort through,' he said haughtily.

'I thought you said you wouldn't be working on this holiday,' she reminded him.

'I did not think I would be, but these things turn up unexpectedly. I will be out tomorrow too,' he informed her.

'Oh, Leon!' Her disappointment was obvious. 'Do you have to?'

The look in his eyes could only be described as one of torment. He wrenched open the door. 'I have to.' He closed the door quietly behind him.

Templar was left staring at the closed door. It was only nine-thirty, what could she do for the rest of the evening? What was there for her to do but go to her room and either read a book or go to bed, which she did unwillingly. Some holiday this was turning out to be!

She read until almost eleven o'clock, finally putting the book down with a sigh. It was a romance and only reminded her of what she hadn't got herself. Leon was acting more unreachable than ever. The new awareness that had sprung up between them wasn't helping either, because no matter how much he denied it, Leon was very much aware of her as a woman. And she was aware of him with every atom of her being, aware of his lean muscular body, of his eyes that could be deeply blue with passion, passion she had aroused in him, of the sensuality of his full lower lip, she was just aware of everything about him. He had only to walk into a room and she felt the electricity of him.

All this was some admission coming from the one person who should hate and despise him. And it was an admission she didn't want to probe too deeply.

She sat propped up against the fluffed-up pillows, biting her lower lip thoughtfully, the only illumination in the room coming from her bedside lamp which she was as yet too lazy to turn out. Besides, she wasn't even remotely tired—how could she be when she had done nothing all day except sit back and take it easy? Keri was very well cared for and didn't really need her twenty-four hours a day any more, which left her with a lot of free time on her hands, free time which Leon didn't seem willing to help her occupy. If only——

She turned sharply as she heard her bedroom door open and close, searching the shadows for her nocturnal visitor. 'Lucy?' She sat up worriedly.

'No,' came the taut reply. 'It is not Lucy.' Leon moved into the soft glow of the bedside lamp, a silk dressing-gown worn over black pyjama trousers, the bareness of his chest pointing to him not wearing the matching jacket. It was so hot here that Templar was surprised he wore anything at all. But perhaps he didn't in the privacy of his own room.

She should have realised it was Leon, he had entered through the communicating door and not the corridor door. It was just that she had never thought he would come into her room like this.

She was very conscious of her limited attire, the thin silk nightdress outlining her firm uptilted breasts. She sank beneath the sheet, although this being silk too really didn't afford her much protection. She looked longingly down at the blanket folded neatly at the bottom of the bed, wishing now that she hadn't felt hot enough to remove it.

'Leon,' she said huskily, gulping nervously.

His eyes gleamed mockingly. 'Obviously.' His face sobered. 'I have come to apologise.'

'A—apologise?' She looked at him apprehensively.

'For my churlish behaviour earlier. I should not have taken out my anger on you, you had done nothing wrong.' He looked haughty, and not in the least repentant.

It felt very strange to be talking to him like this in the intimacy of her bedroom, and yet he had a perfect right to be here. He was her husband, and a husband was perfectly within his rights to visit his wife's bedroom.

She shrugged now. 'You were angry about something. Who better than me to vent your anger on?'

Leon smiled slightly, a softening of his harsh features that was totally unexpected. 'If you are trying to make me feel guilty I think it only fair to tell you that you have succeeded.'

Templar felt some of the tension begin to leave her body. 'I didn't mean to make you feel guilty. I just wanted you to know that I understood your wish to strike out at someone. I'm the obvious person, as you would be in my case.'

He was watching her closely. 'You can be so serious for one so young,' he remarked calmly. 'I forget at times just how young you are. You always appear cool and composed, always perfectly groomed in every way.'

She put up a rueful hand to her ruffled auburn hair, conscious of her face completely free of make-up. 'Not right now I'm not,' she said shyly.

His eyes widened as he looked at her. 'You appear no less beautiful,' his voice was deep and husky. He moved closer to her. 'You are very attractive, Templar—too attractive for my peace of mind. How am I supposed to sleep with you in bed in the next room to mine?' The last came out in a groan. He came to sit on the bed, one hand moving up to caress her creamy cheek. 'Like a flame you draw me ever so close, like a child I fall for your fascination, uncaring if I get burnt.'

Templar reacted to the tremor of his voice, her body feeling like an aching void that needed Leon's possession of her to make her complete. It was as if the last five days had never been, as if they were once again on the beach, their bodies drawn together despite the fevered dictates of their brains. She made an involuntary move towards him and that was their undoing.

Her capitulation was all Leon needed to make him lose control, his arms reaching out to pull her against the hardness of his muscular chest. For long agonising moments he gazed into her passion-filled eyes, until at last, with a deep shuddering groan, he moved down to possess her lips.

He had never kissed her before and Templar wasn't quite sure what it would be like. But as could be expected, Leon took complete control, gently prising her lips apart with the tip of his tongue, the kiss deepening, the feelings he aroused in her almost too much to bear.

He laid her gently back against the cool sheets, discarding his silk dressing-gown in one fluid movement, before sliding on to the bed beside her, their bodies fused together in aching desperation. He looked down at her with glazed brilliant blue eyes. 'I want you, Templar,' it was a groan from deep within him. 'I want you!'

Templar was aware only of his hard body pressed against her, not needing his impassioned words to tell her of his need of her. His completely male smell invaded her nostrils and his hair felt damp to her touch, evidence of his recent shower. 'Leon, I——'

His face was buried in her scented throat as he rained kisses on her soft smooth skin. 'Do not speak, Templar, only feel. Feel the electricity that exists between us, of the pleasures our bodies could so easily give each other.'

'But, Leon——' She fought to bring him back to sanity. But her own senses clamoured against such thoughts, as her body arched against the hardness of his, for the moment nothing but their desire seeming important to either of them.

'*Feel*, Templar,' he urged.

She felt. Her whole body was alive to his touch and she shuddered with feeling as one of his hands pushed aside her nightdress to travel slowly up over her body to cup one breast possessively, feeling the nipple rise and flower to his caress. She gasped at the feelings of sensual pleasure this evoked in her body, pushing herself hard against those probing fingers.

It was as if a dam had burst between them, Leon shaking with as yet suppressed desire for her and she but a trembling pliant body in his arms. He gently pushed aside the thin strap to her nightgown, and when the material remained adamantly in place his hand momentarily left her breast to hold the scooped neckline and wrench the nightgown from her body in one sharp tug.

Templar's eyes widened at her nakedness. 'Oh, please, Leon! No ...'

For a moment his eyes gleamed devilishly down at her before he bent his dark head, his lips claiming the tip of one rosy breast. 'Oh, yes,' he murmured almost inaudibly, his soft warm breath across her breast a sensuous pleasure in itself. 'Oh yes, my darling,' he repeated passionately soft.

His lips and hands claimed her body once again and she threw back her head in mounting passion. Never before had she felt this increasing sexual excitement, never before had any man touched her body so intimately, but there was no thought of refusal on her lips.

Her hands moved down his chest, over his taut flat stomach to the single button that held on the only piece of clothing that now lay between them. But Leon's hand moved to stop her before she could complete her task. 'Not yet, Templar,' his voice was husky with the emotion it took him to speak, all his attention fixed on retaining control for several minutes longer.

Her green eyes widened pleadingly. 'Please, Leon!' she begged desperately, but for completely the opposite reason to her last pleading. This time she cried out for his possession of her, for his full taking of her roused body.

He moved up and away from her, leaning on his elbow to watch her through glazed unfocusing eyes. 'I want to look at you first, to know every inch of this delectable body of yours, not take you at the first rising of passion.' His voice had lowered to a seductive whisper. 'And after I have explored all there is of you to explore I want you to do the same to me. Do you understand, Templar? I want you to be more excited by me than by any other man who has ever possessed you. I want you never to want another man as long as you live. For me to be the only man you can ever respond to, wanting to be touched and made love to only by me.'

Templar felt panic begin to rise inside her. 'You can't mean what you're saying!'

He gave a throaty triumphant laugh. 'All I am saying is that I intend to make love to you tonight until you can think of no one but me, want no one but me. Is that so difficult to understand?' He himself released the button to his pyjama trousers, shedding them in one unhurried movement, moving back to her side until their naked bodies were so close together they were almost one. Almost . . .

For one terribly satisfying moment Templar felt herself respond to his hard nakedness, found pleasure in the muscled roughness of his skin against her. Then sensibility took over and she fought against him for all she was worth.

His eyes narrowed as she began to struggle. 'What are you doing now?' he asked sharply. 'Why are you fighting me?'

'Because—because you're acting like that animal you once accused me of thinking you. An animal!' she spat the word at him, feeling a momentary weakness as he moved away from her. 'You only want me to prove your manhood, to prove how omnipotent you are. Well, you aren't going to do it this way. I want you to get out of my bedroom. Get out now!'

Leon moved off the bed at once, standing like a Greek god in the golden glow of the lamplight, unconcerned with his own nakedness. His eyes held nothing but contempt for her as she still lay in her wanton position amongst the crumpled bedclothes. Her hurried movements to cover herself only increased the contempt in that gaze. 'A little late for that, would you not agree?' He didn't have his feelings under control yet, his eyes still that deep blue they always were when he was aroused to passion.

She looked at him resentfully. 'You started this!'

'You did not exactly fight me off!'

'I—I tried.'

'No, you did not! You call those half-hearted protests fighting me off?'

Templar sat up, the sheet wrapped around her shoulders, her hair a tangled curtain down her back from his fevered touch. 'I didn't ask you in here. No one *invited* you!'

He picked up his discarded clothing, not bothering to put it back on. 'Your eyes invite me every time you look at me. I could do no other than respond to that look. Tonight you pushed me too far. I warned you it would happen, but it appears you did not heed that warning. When I came in here to see you you lay there looking at me over the top of that sheet, invitation in every line of your body.'

'I did not!'

'Yes, you did.' He ran a tired hand over his eyes. 'I must be mad. God, I have to get out of here!'

'I wish you would,' she said quietly.

His eyes were tortured as he looked at her. 'So much for my noble words of the other day! This will happen time and time again if I do not get a control on my desire for you. I will go now. And please try to believe me this time when I say I will try to see it does not happen again.'

'That's all I ask,' she said brokenly, not even sure if she meant it, but doubting it very much.

CHAPTER SEVEN

TEMPLAR felt dazed when she awoke the next morning, almost as if what had happened between Leon and herself had only been a dream. But her nightgown lying ripped to shreds on the floor at the foot of the bed told her that it had been stark reality. Leon had entered her bedroom last night and they had so nearly consummated this sham of a marriage.

She admitted that she had responded wantonly, but what had happened to all that cool control Leon had assured her he possessed? It had been as nothing as soon as he touched her, their senses reeling, their bodies crying out for assuagement.

She had lain awake long after he had left her, reliving every passionate, nerve-tingling moment, and cursing herself for being a fool. She loved Leon! It was as simple as that. Only it wasn't simple at all. She loved him, and like any normal female in love she wanted him to make love to her day and night until she couldn't even think straight.

And it had so nearly happened, so nearly been true that it was frightening. That Leon desired her just as desperately was obvious, and that made the situation between them positively explosive. How long could they deny these feelings, how long before they gave in to the senses and not logic? Living together in such close proximity, it was going to be pure hell to fight these feelings, but fight them she must.

The one thing that had brought her to her senses the previous night was Leon's vow to make her forget the other men who had possessed her. It hadn't so much been the fact that the words were insulting—they were no worse than some of the other things he had called her in the past. No, it was the realisation that possession by Leon would prove possession by no one else, and that couldn't be allowed to happen.

God, what hell had she created for herself? Why did she have to fall in love with him, why couldn't she have gone on disliking him? It had all been so much easier that way. Now she had to live with him, yearn for him, long for him, and know that it was an impossibility. It was like hell on earth. But it would have to be her own private hell; Leon must never know, never be allowed to even guess at her feelings for him.

She climbed miserably out of bed, hiding her nakedness with her silk wrap. These thoughts were all well and good, but right now she had to get herself dressed and go downstairs and face him. And at the moment she wasn't sure she could do it. Perhaps a nice cool shower might relax her, and it might help to wake her up. She had cried so much the night before that her eyes felt as if she had sand under the lids.

A hurried glance in the bathroom mirror assured her that she looked as bad as she felt. How could she face Leon looking like this?—she looked ghastly. She would just have to hope he didn't look at her too closely.

A quick shower and some extensive work on her make-up and she looked somewhere near presentable. She hesitated about entering the dining-room, but forced herself to do so, only to find the one person she was nervous of meeting conspicuous by his absence. Lucy and the baby were playing on the sand outside the open french doors, but the dining-room itself was empty.

Lucy looked up and smiled as she noticed her entrance. 'Good morning, Mrs Marcose.'

Templar returned the smile vaguely. 'Lucy, I'm sorry I'm a little late down this morning. Has Keri had her breakfast?'

'Oh yes, we ate with Mr Marcose quite a long time ago. He thought it best not to disturb you, that perhaps you needed the rest.'

She blushed, hoping Lucy wouldn't be able to guess the reason for her embarrassment. She had lain awake so long the evening before thinking and dreaming of things that could never be that it had been very late when she finally drifted off to sleep. And she had paid for it by oversleeping this morning, rising two hours later than her normal eight o'clock.

'Yes, yes, perhaps I did.' She helped herself to a cup of strong black coffee, the thought of food nauseating to her. 'And has Leon—my husband, has he gone down to the beach?'

The young girl frowned. 'Mr Marcose isn't here. He went out about an hour ago.'

'Went out?' Her movements were jerky with lack of sleep, her nerves shattered by her recent discovery of love for her husband.

'Yes.' Lucy picked up the crawling Keri. 'He said that you would know where he had gone.'

Pain filled Templar's already shadowed eyes. 'Is that all the message he left?'

Lucy was concerned with the struggling baby and so didn't notice her distress. 'He also said he wouldn't be back for dinner, but he said you would probably have already realised that.'

Templar turned away to finish off her coffee. So that was Leon's answer to the total awareness that had sprung up between them, avoidance of her wherever possible. She wished she found it so easy to dismiss him, was able to turn her emotions off so easily. She found it hard enough concentrating on simple everyday things, let alone going off to a business meeting as if everything in her life was as normal as it had been yesterday morning.

She felt she would never be normal again, never be able to forget her excitement in Leon's arms, her desire to please him. But obviously he felt no such reserve, calmly going off to his meeting as if nothing had happened between them. Her shyness about facing him again hadn't been necessary, at least, not yet. She would still have to face him this evening—when he eventually returned.

'Your husband told me to look after Keri today, Mrs Marcose,' Lucy looked at her uncertainly. 'Is that all right with you?'

At least someone in this household bothered to consult her wishes! 'That will be fine,' she nodded agreement. 'I—er—I was thinking of going for a walk along the beach anyway.'

'Very well, Mrs Marcose. I'll just go and collect Keri's things for the beach.'

'I'll wait here and walk down with you.'

She left Keri and Lucy on the beach, strolling in the direction of Neil Adams' villa. It couldn't be that far away, not if he had swum over, and he had said he would see her today, so why shouldn't she be the one to visit him? She felt she needed a change of scenery at the moment, complete removal from anything that reminded her of Leon.

Neil Adams' villa was further than she had imagined, at least two miles away. But she knew she had the right place because Neil and several other men were lounging on the beach in front of the villa. She felt rather shy about announcing her presence now she was actually here, but after that walk she needed a long cool drink.

Some of the men were getting ready to go in for a swim and Neil spotted her standing some distance away from them as he too stood up. 'Templar!' He looked pleased to see her. 'Come on over.'

She was introduced to several of his companions before he took her up to the villa for the much-needed drink. 'You have quite a few friends staying with you,' she remarked, her thirst assuaged by the cool lime juice.

Neil laughed. 'That isn't all my guests, a couple of the men and three of the girls have gone into Nice shopping. There are twelve of us here altogether,' he revealed.

It was a large villa and Templar estimated it could house much more than twelve. 'What do you do all day?' she asked.

He shrugged. 'We swim, sunbathe, snorkel. Actually six of my guests aren't actually here on holiday, they're here to work. Bob over there is the man with the camera, Paul represents the company involved, Sheila is one of the models, and the other three are the girls who have gone shopping.'

Templar had herself been on a couple of jobs like this, although not in quite such luxurious surroundings. The models must be some of the more popular ones to have landed a job like this one. She had recognised Sheila instantly, a beautiful brunette with blue flashing eyes; she was often on the front of magazines.

'It sounds as if they're having fun,' she commented.

'Oh, they are. But I'll be glad of a little peace and quiet. They leave in three days' time. When do you go?'

She shrugged. 'Leon hasn't said yet. It all depends on him.'

'Then maybe we'll be able to meet when the crowd have departed. Perhaps you can persuade Leon to come over too?'

'I don't know. He—he doesn't know we've met.'

'No,' Neil said thoughtfully, 'I don't suppose he does. Oh well, perhaps I can drop over one day and announce myself. We've never been the best of friends, just acquaintances, but nevertheless I don't think he would be unsociable if I invited him over.'

Templar wasn't so sure, Leon could be downright arrogant if he chose to be. 'You can try it,' she agreed. 'I'd love to come.'

Neil replenished her glass for her. 'Where's the baby today?'

She smiled gently at thought of Keri. 'She's with a young girl we have to look after her. Being Greek Leon doesn't think I should be with her all the time, they usually employ full-time nannies in their households. I don't actually approve of it myself, but Leon can be very obstinate about these things.'

He grinned. 'I can imagine. Did you bring a costume with you?'

'I have it on under my denims and tee-shirt. If you could let me use one of your towels?'

Neil stood up. 'I'll go and get you one.'

'Fine.' She removed her top clothing while waiting for him, revealing a minute bikini in a becoming rust colour. Her golden tan was shown to full advantage against its muted colour and her slender curvaceous body looked very attractive in the bright sunshine, her legs long and shapely.

'Wow!' Neil handed her the gaily flowered towel. 'You're beautiful!'

She blushed. 'Do you usually make those sort of re-marks to married ladies?'

'If they look like you—yes, otherwise—no. What a loss to the modelling world you are. Our loss is Leon's gain,' he sighed.

'Yes.'

He quirked an eyebrow at her. 'You don't sound as if you agree with me.'

'*I* may do,' she laughed nervously. 'But I'm not sure Leon would.'

'I'm sure he would,' he disagreed, putting out a hand towards her. 'Come on, let's swim, it's too good a day to waste.'

And it was. They swam together for half an hour or more before lying on the beach, their conversation just seeming to flow. They had so much in common, often knowing the same people, that they found they had a lot to talk about. So it was no surprise to Templar when she saw it was already five-thirty, time she returned to the villa.

She put her denims and tee-shirt back on over her sun-dried bikini, smiling regretfully at the end of her visit, fresh colour in her cheeks and a happy glow to her eyes. It had done her good to be with the uncom-plicated Neil, but now she had to return to her world of cold politeness with Leon. If only he weren't always so chilling towards her! But last night he hadn't been——

She cut off these thoughts before they could be al-lowed to destroy her again. Last night was over and best forgotten. 'I have to leave now, Neil,' she told him, handing him the towel she had used.

'Stay to dinner,' he encouraged. 'You refused lunch, so you can't refuse dinner too.'

Templar laughed at his logic. 'I refused lunch because I wasn't hungry. I have to get back to the villa for dinner.'

'Will Leon be there?'

'Well, no, but I——'

'Then you're staying here,' he said determinedly. 'I insist.'

She looked down at her crumpled clothing. 'I can't sit down to dinner dressed like this.'

Neil sensed her wavering and pushed home his advantage. 'I'll drive you home so you can change. And we don't sit down to dinner here, it's usually cold buffet in the lounge. People just wander in and help themselves throughout the evening.'

Templar hesitated. This casual way of dining would suit her, she felt shy about meeting too many people formally at one time. And Leon wouldn't be home for dinner. Why shouldn't she stay here, it would be much better than eating alone as she had last night.

'All right,' she gave in. 'But I would like to go home and check on the baby, and I may as well change at the same time.'

'Fine. I'll just get my car keys from the lounge.' Within two minutes he was back, the car keys jangling in his hand. 'Ready?' he smiled.

'Ready,' she agreed, glancing uncertainly at his guests as they still lazed on the beach. 'Ought we to tell them where we've gone?'

Neil grinned. 'Oh, no. They won't even miss us.' He opened the car door for her to get in, a low white sports car that was ideal for this sort of weather with its canvas roof, lowered now so as to allow the wind to rush through the hair. 'We're very informal here,' he explained. 'Everyone does what they want to do.'

It took them less than five minutes to reach the villa,

but it would have taken Templar much longer on foot. She invited him in for a drink while she showered and changed, hurrying to her room.

Lucy was just completing Keri's bath when she entered the nursery a couple of minutes later. Templar took the baby into her arms, feeling quite guilty about leaving her all day. But she shouldn't do really, this was the first day she had had to herself for weeks.

'Has she been good?' She looked at Lucy.

The young girl smiled. 'Isn't she always?'

Templar laughed. 'No!'

'She has been today.' Lucy tidied away the things from the bath, drying off the plastic duck that had been bobbing about in the bath water until a few minutes ago.

'Has—has Mr Marcose called at all?' Templar asked casually, putting on Keri's nightdress.

'No.' Lucy was too preoccupied or she would have noticed her sigh of relief. 'Were you expecting a call?'

'Oh, no,' she answered hastily. 'I just wondered if he'd changed his mind about dinner. I'm going out myself, you see, and I didn't want him to arrive home only to find me out.'

'Oh well, he hasn't called as yet, but if he does I'll tell him you're out.'

She kissed Keri lovingly on the cheek, smiling at the baby's chuckles. 'Off you go to bed, young lady, and I'll pop in and see you when I get home.' She gave Keri to Lucy. 'I shouldn't be too late, probably before Mr Marcose arrives home anyway.'

She hurried to her room, showering the salt water away from her body quickly before donning a buttercup-yellow cocktail dress, brushing her hair till it shone before applying a light lip-gloss. She didn't want to keep Neil waiting any longer than was necessary.

He stood up with a smile as she came into the room, putting down the magazine he had been idly flicking through. 'You look lovely. Are you ready to leave?'

'Oh, yes. Keri's fine, I needn't have worried.'

'They tell me mothers are always the same,' he sympathised. 'I suppose she's gone to bed now?'

'That's right.'

'Where all good little girls should be,' he said softly, the look in his eyes teasing her.

'You're flirting with me again,' she laughed. 'Have you forgotten I'm married?'

He helped her back into the car. 'I like flirting with married ladies, it's much safer than with the single ones.'

'It is if the jealous husband doesn't find out,' she laughed glowingly at him, the coastal wind blowing through her hair.

'But he's safely away on business.'

She frowned. 'Who is?'

'Why, Leon, of course.'

'Oh, of course.' Templar blushed. 'But I can't see him in the role of jealous husband.'

'I can. Perhaps you just haven't given him reason to be yet. That Greek temperament of his can be quite fiery on occasion.'

Oh, she knew that, she had witnessed his temper numerous times, had been the cause of it more times than she cared to remember. But she didn't want to think of Leon tonight, she wanted to forget for a few hours that she was married to that enigmatic man, to forget her newly realised love for him.

And she did for a couple of hours, deliberately joining in with all the laughter and chatter that existed in abundance between eight people bent on enjoying themselves. The shoppers of Nice hadn't yet returned, although Neil felt sure they would soon find them as they danced and played records on the beach.

As the only two girls of the party she and Sheila found themselves the centre of attraction, finally crying off dancing altogether and insisting that they were exhausted. Bob, the earnest young photographer, produced a guitar and began to accompany himself as he sang several folk songs. They were songs that were well-known and the others soon joined in on the chorus lines.

These were the sort of parties Templar had enjoyed before the advent of Keri into her life, gay lighthearted parties that had always resulted in a little harmless flirtation between the sexes. And so it was that in the dying sunset she found herself leaning against Neil's shoulder, the two of them happily singing along with the melodious and talented Bob.

They were laughing happily together when she sensed other eyes watching them, disapproving eyes that she hardly dared to turn and meet. Her face paled and all humour left it as she met the blazing grey eyes of her husband.

The other girls staying at this luxurious villa had returned from their shopping, and Templar was dismayed to see that Rachel Winter was one of them. And she was clinging very firmly to Leon's arm, a look of absolute possession on her smug face. She looked like a cat who had got the cream and Templar felt her temper rising jealously.

Neil had also seen the newcomers and his firm grip on her arm held her at his side as she would have made a move towards the other couple. 'Calm down, Templar,' he warned softly. 'A scene is just what Rachel would enjoy.'

She knew he was right and yet the anger remained. She saw Leon's steely gaze flicker across Neil's hold on her and saw his head snap back arrogantly. His obvious show of anger only added to her own and she turned away from him furiously.

Neil gave her what appeared to be a natural smile but which she could see was only for her benefit. His next words confirmed her belief. 'Don't show her you care, Templar,' he advised, that smile still on his face. 'She'd love that.'

She did her best to take his advice and relax, but was ever conscious of her husband and Rachel Winter now helping themselves to a drink from the makeshift bar. 'But that's my husband, Neil,' she said brokenly. 'I can't just ignore the fact that he's here with another woman.'

'This is the first time it's ever happened?'

'Doesn't my reaction tell you so? Oh, I knew things weren't right between us, but I never expected this. I feel—I feel betrayed, let down.'

'*How* wrong are things between you?'

Tears filled her eyes. 'Very wrong. In fact, the only thing keeping the marriage together is Keri. We both love her.'

'So I've witnessed. But if things are that bad between you ...' he shook his head. 'Well, Rachel is— she's very attractive, and totally immoral. And Leon is —well, he's a man.'

Oh, she knew that! She had had it proved very effectively last night. She sighed. 'I know what you're trying to say, Neil, but finding the reason for his behaviour doesn't make it any easier to accept.'

He put his hand over hers. 'I know that, love. I'm just trying to explain that men are different from women—Now don't look like that, I mean apart from the obvious differences. To a man sex is an important part of his life.'

'And if he isn't getting what he wants at home then he'll get it elsewhere,' she finished for him.

Neil looked uncomfortable. 'Something like that. And Rachel isn't averse to an affair.'

'I know that. She told me as much herself.'

'*She* told you?' He looked astounded.

'Mm, she came to the house with Leon a few weeks ago,' she admitted reluctantly.

'My God!' he shook his head disbelievingly. 'He actually brought her to your home? And didn't you realise what was going on then?'

She wanted to turn and look at Leon again but didn't know if she could stand that twisting pain in her heart every time she saw him with that woman. 'I—' she choked over the words. 'I asked Leon about it and he—he denied it, emphatically.'

'What did you expect him to do? Good grief, Templar! You aren't that stupid that you imagine he would calmly own up to something like that? You can't be that naïve!'

'I'm growing up very fast married to Leon.'

He looked past her and over her shoulder. 'Well, now's the time to show just how grown up you really are,' he said softly. 'They're coming over.'

Templar felt herself stiffen as she sensed Leon and that—that *woman* behind her, standing up with a helping hand from Neil. She brushed the sand from her dress, delaying the moment when she threw back her head to meet the furious onslaught of the anger in her husband's face.

He was looking very attractive in a cream lounge suit and coffee-brown shirt opened casually at the throat.

He wore his clothes with the casual arrogance that drew attention to his lean frame without any conscious effort on his part. But it was his face that caught and held her attention now, the rapier sharpness of his eyes and the contemptuous twist to his lips.

'Neil,' he nodded sharply to the other man before looking at her again. 'I did not realise you were coming here this evening,' he said distantly. 'Otherwise we could have come together.'

So it was to be pretence, was it, even though the four of them knew the true circumstances behind them both being here with other people. Leon intended to act as if he hadn't come here with another woman, with the woman who had been his mistress all the time they had been married, and maybe before that—Templar didn't know. She would let him have his way for the moment, but once they were back in their own villa it would be another story. Now she had reason to throw some accusations of her own, instead of always being on the receiving end.

She gave a bright smile. 'I had no idea myself until this afternoon when Neil invited me.'

Again he looked at the other man. 'I was not aware that you knew my wife.'

'Well, I——'

'We've known each other for ages,' Templar cut in. And it did seem a long time since their first meeting of yesterday, so much had happened in that short time. She had discovered that loving Leon could be a painful thing, causing a hurt that reached far within her. This wasn't how she had wanted them to meet again after last night, not this cold conversation that made a mockery of everything that had happened the previous evening. And their mutual suspicion would not help their relationship one little bit, she realised that, even if she couldn't stop it.

Rachel seemed to feel she had been ignored long enough, her hand on Leon's arm a show of possession rather than affection. 'Leon and I went shopping this morning, didn't we, darling?' she purred the words at him.

Leon's mouth tightened and he looked sharply at Templar. 'We met briefly at the shops,' he amended.

'And then you took me to lunch,' she persisted, obviously determined Templar should know the full extent of their day together.

'Yes,' he said shortly.

The knife twisted more tightly in Templar's chest. Leon had gone more or less straight from her own arms to this woman's—and no doubt his passion had been suitably assuaged by her, unlike her own efforts.

'How did the business meeting go, darling?' she asked him pointedly, watching as a slight flush darkened his skin at her easy use of the endearment.

'It was completed much sooner than I had imagined it would be,' he answered stiffly.

Oh yes, she could imagine that any business he had to deal with would be quickly despatched when he had the beautiful and willing Rachel waiting for him. *If* there had ever been any business to deal with, which she doubted.

'I see,' she said sweetly. 'What a pity you didn't let me know.'

'It did not seem necessary.'

'No, I don't suppose it did,' she answered dully, turning to look at Rachel, ignoring the spiteful look of satisfaction on her face. 'It's nice to see you again, Rachel.'

'Is it?' Rachel returned softly.

Templar wanted to hit back at the challenge in the other girl's words, wanted to shout and scream her own possession of Leon's affections, but she knew this to be untrue. He couldn't even like her very much if he could invite his mistress along on their holiday.

And so she didn't answer the other girl at all, ignoring the remark altogether. 'Neil was just about to take me home,' her eyes signalled her desperation to him.

Her words caused Leon to look even more detached, his grey-blue eyes narrowing dangerously. 'Now that I am here I am perfectly capable of taking my own wife home.'

'Oh, but—' she went to protest, but was silenced by the anger on Leon's face.

Rachel looked up at Leon poutingly. 'But we've only just got here, darling. Surely you don't have to leave so soon?'

'I think it would be as well,' he said softly.

'Lunch tomorrow?' she persisted, her blue eyes seductively inviting, her pouting lips slightly parted.

'I am not sure——'

'That sounds like a good idea,' Neil interrupted happily. 'You'll be able to bring Templar with you. I wasn't quite sure about whether I would be able to pick her up, my car has to go in for a service tomorrow. But if you're coming over, Leon, you'll be able to bring her.'

His words implied that they had already arranged to meet for lunch tomorrow and Templar felt grateful for his moral support. She wasn't sure Leon felt too happy about it, his steely gaze once more flickering inflexibly over the other man.

He turned to look at her now. 'Is that suitable for you?' he asked her curtly.

She knew by the look on his face that she was supposed to refuse to come at all, but a devil inside her urged her on. She faced him defiantly. He might have

a mistress, but she certainly wasn't going to be seen to
encourage his affair. 'I think that's an excellent idea,'
she agreed.

'Very well,' he nodded abruptly. 'Will one o'clock be
suitable?' he asked their host.

'One o'clock will be fine. I'll see you tomorrow,
Templar.' All the time he was talking he drew her
further away from the other couple, until they were
some distance away. 'Keep your chin up, love. He is
your husband, after all.'

She glanced back to where Rachel was holding Leon
in deep conversation, her face animated, her eyes glowing. 'Try telling that to Rachel,' she said dryly.

'Things aren't always what they seem. Give Leon a
chance to explain.'

She did, all the way back to the villa, but he sat
silently at her side, his mouth a thin straight line. The
silence was oppressive in the car, his anger a tangible
thing. But why should he be angry? She was the one
who had to witness her own humiliation when he had
arrived with his mistress on his arm.

Once inside the villa she could stand it no longer,
opening her mouth to speak. 'Leon, I——'

'You will be silent!' he snapped. 'At least wait until
we reach the privacy of our own rooms before you cause
a scene. One of the staff could walk in here at any
moment.'

'And we mustn't have that, must we?' she taunted
recklessly. 'I have to be humiliated in front of all those
people, but your staff mustn't be allowed to witness us
having an argument!'

His eyes were glacial. 'I said be quiet! We will go to
your room and talk.'

'My room ...?' Her look was apprehensive.

Leon gave a taunting smile. 'You need not fear

seduction from me. I am not in the mood right now to
make love to you or any other woman.'

'Because you already have!'

His face darkened with an anger that was frightening. 'We will go to your room!'

CHAPTER EIGHT

ONCE in her bedroom Templar switched on the two illuminating side-lamps, turning defensively to face Leon as he closed the door quietly behind him. 'So we're here in my room. What now?'

'Now I want to know what you were doing at Neil Adams' villa?' his eyes were watchful.

'You want to know what I——!' She laughed, her voice cracking angrily. 'Don't you think the fact that you have been out all day with another woman is of more importance? That you have been making love to her, that you turn up at someone else's home with her? I think that's much more important.'

'Your accusations are unjust——'

'Are they? *Darling*!'

'You have no foundation——'

'I have, damn you!' her voice rose shrilly. 'All the time you insisted that I needed a holiday when all along the real reason you wanted to come here was so that you could be with your girl-friend. You disgust me!'

His dark skin had taken on a greyish tinge. 'So I disgust you, do I? You are a cold little bitch who has taunted me beyond endurance, forced me into the arms of another woman for the satisfaction which you deny me! And you say I disgust you! Do you have any idea what you did to me last night, the torture you put me through into the early hours of this morning?'

'Until you could get to your mistress and assuage your lust!' she spat the words at him.

'And if I did?' he too lost his temper. 'Can I be blamed for that, for finding what satisfaction I can with who I can?' He lifted his shoulders, a purely Greek gesture.

His admission hurt her unbearably. 'Yes, you can be blamed, when you deny me the same satisfaction! I have the same feelings as you, the same bodily longings. Oh, but I forgot, women shouldn't feel like that, should they? I should meekly sit back and feel relieved that you aren't bothering me with your unwanted attentions.' She shook her head. 'It doesn't work that way. Women have the same feelings, we just aren't allowed to show them the way men are.'

'Is that why you were in Neil Adams' arms a few minutes ago? Were you after assuagement to your own desires?' He glared his distaste at her.

Templar glared at him defiantly. 'What makes you think I haven't already found it? I went to Neil's villa before lunch.'

'My God!' Leon muttered, his accent thickening with the deepening of his emotions. 'Is this what it has come to, both of us finding our pleasures elsewhere?'

Suddenly all the fight went out of her and she found she couldn't lie any more, no matter how much he had hurt her with his duplicity. 'I haven't done that, Leon. I wouldn't—I couldn't——'

His eyes widened at her words, studying the auburn sheen of her bent head. 'Are you trying to tell me that the marriage vows we made in that cold impersonal register office mean something to you?'

'Where they were made makes no difference to their meaning,' she shrugged. 'I happen to believe in the sanctity of marriage. You've just made a mockery of all that.'

'And if I have not?'

'But you—you have! Rachel and you, you——'

'We have done nothing which I could not freely tell you about. I am not saying Rachel would not like us to, in that respect you were right about her, but I am afraid I am incapable of becoming her lover.'

'But you just told me——'

'I told you what you expected to hear. You aroused these passions, Templar, only you can satisfy me. You have me wound up so tight I saw everything through a red haze when I arrived at Neil's tonight. I felt murderous when I saw his arm round your shoulders.' His body slumped and he ran a tired hand through his already windswept hair. 'I could have struck out at him and not cared who witnessed my anger.'

'I don't understand, Leon. This evening I thought you—Rachel acted as if——'

Leon sighed. 'Acted is the right word. She did it deliberately, and fool that I am, I let her.' He sat down on her bed with a sigh. 'You are ruining me, Templar.'

'I haven't done anything!'

'You do not need to. This marriage is not going to work, not as it is.'

Templar felt her heart lurch at the look of passion in his eyes, and her legs felt weak. 'Leon, we can't——'

'Why can we not?' he cut in harshly. 'I cannot live like this any longer. I have been attracted to you ever since I first saw you in that tiny flat you lived in, but now it is so bad that I cannot even see other women. I want no other woman, Templar. I have to have you, do you not see that?'

She longed to go into his arms, to let him do as he had said the night before, make love to her for hours on end until she could think of nothing but him. But she couldn't do that, it couldn't be allowed to happen.

Greater intimacy between them could only lead to her losing Keri and consequently Leon himself. But her longing for him was made all the worse by the knowledge that he too desired her and wanted her as she wanted him.

'It wouldn't work, Leon.' Her voice broke.

'Why would it not?' he asked fiercely. 'Surely it is only natural that as man and wife we should——'

'No!' She hadn't meant to protest so loudly, but the word came out almost as a shout. 'I—I can't. Don't you see that?'

'You find me repulsive?'

She couldn't meet the passionate intensity of his eyes. 'You must know I don't. Last night——'

'Last night you responded to me. You felt the same desire I did. I should not have spoken, I should just have loved you. I tell myself that the feelings I have towards you are wrong, and I know that you feel this too, but——'

'No, no, I don't,' she denied hotly, sitting beside him on the bed to clutch his arm to her side. 'It isn't wrong, Leon. That isn't why I can't—why I can't let you make love to me. One day I'll be able to explain my reasons.' One day, when Keri was old enough not to be hurt by what she would reveal. 'One day, Leon.'

'One day! What good is that to me when I want you now?' He gripped her shoulders with strong fingers. 'I want you now, Templar!'

Her protests were swallowed up by his hungry lips, the touching of his warm body against hers drugging to the senses. They lay close together on top of the bed, Templar unable to fight her longing for his kisses.

Her hands moved up the strength of his chest, holding him against her, her lips moving invitingly beneath his. He dragged his mouth away to bury his face in her neck, his tongue probing the sensitive area beneath her ear-lobe.

Her head thrown back in submission, she hardly noticed as he moved one strong hand across her back to release the zip to her dress, slipping the shoulder-strap down one side to caress her creamy skin.

'Let me stay tonight, Templar,' he begged. 'Let me stay here with you.'

She wanted him to. Oh God, how she wanted him to! But how could she let it happen, was one night in his arms worth spending the rest of her life alone, without him or Keri to love? He was a proud man and she had no doubt that when he found out the truth about her he would throw her out without a qualm.

So far she had managed not to lie to him, but she thought it was only a lie that would save her now. She forced herself to lie passive in his arms, not to fight him but not to respond either.

He raised his dark head from the shadow of her breasts. 'What is it? What is the matter?'

There could be no doubt of Leon's arousal, it was there in the firm outline of his body and the husky tone of his voice. His eyes were glazed with as yet suppressed desire for her and she knew that a simple no would not suffice to stop him this time, that she would have to be deliberately cruel if he were not to make her his right now.

She shook her head regretfully. 'I can't do it, Leon. I can't do it to you.'

Leon made an effort to think straight. 'What is it you cannot do to me? If you are shy——'

She wasn't shy, far from it, when she was in his arms. She was a wanton then, wanting only his lips and the caresses that aroused them both to the point of forgetting everything but each other.

'It isn't that,' she denied.

He resumed kissing her throat. 'Then what is it?' he asked between kisses.

'I can't let you do this because I—because I would only be using you as a substitute.'

His head snapped back, the passion slowly fading from his intense blue eyes. 'As a substitute?' he repeated in a stunned voice. 'For whom?'

Templar took a deep breath, making herself say the words but hating herself for lying to him. 'For Alex, of course,' she said quietly.

For one heart-rendering moment there was no reaction to her words and then Leon sprang off the bed as if she had struck him. Anger shone in his now slate grey eyes as he buttoned his shirt with jerky movements.

'Leon, I——'

'Do not say another word!' he ground out between clenched teeth. 'So all this time I have just been a substitute for my brother? God, you are a bitch!'

She was shaking with reaction, his anger as bad as she had thought it would be. But it had been the only way! 'You're so much like him,' she added chokingly. 'It could be no other way.'

Leon's movements stopped and he looked at her with narrowed eyes. 'You have said this before, but we were nothing alike.'

She could imagine they hadn't been in temperament —someone as forceful as Leon would have terrified Tiffany. She would never have been able to cope with someone like him. 'Not in temperament, perhaps. But in looks ... Every time I look at you I'm reminded of him.' She kneaded her hands together. 'So you see, if I allowed you to make love to me I would only be doing it because I could imagine you were Alex. It wouldn't be fair to you.'

He straightened his jacket as he slipped it over his shoulders. 'I see,' he nodded his head, his look grim. 'So you really did love Alex?'

'I—Yes! You were right about me in other ways, though. About the baby,' she explained hurriedly at his darkening look. 'I knew Alex was Keri's father.' She did now anyway. 'But when she was born she looked like any other baby. I didn't stand a chance of convincing Alex he was the father.'

'Because he knew you for what you were!' he bit out angrily.

'That's right,' she admitted. 'I'm exactly what you always said I was. But I did love Alex, that's why I kept Keri.'

'And you cannot let me make love to you because I remind you of him?'

'That's right,' she sighed. 'You understand?'

'Oh yes, I understand. You think us very much alike?'

She nodded. 'Very.'

'Very well. I will see you tomorrow. I have no wish to be a substitute for anyone, especially my brother.' He nodded distantly, quietly leaving the room without another word.

Breakfast was a silent affair except for Keri's murmurings. Leon wasn't so much angry as preoccupied, and Templar was far too nervous to say a word. All this time she had managed to get through without lying, and last night she had told so many lies she just couldn't believe she was actually hearing herself speak.

How Leon must hate her now, how she hated herself too. He hadn't been too proud to admit his need of her and she had rebuffed him in the most painful way possible, declaring her preference for his dead brother.

But his reaction had been a little strange. He had been angry at first, and then he had gone strangely thoughtful. And this morning he wasn't deliberately ignoring her, in fact he had been very polite to her since she had come down to the breakfast table.

He put down his newspaper now, the slight smile on his face for the baby fading as he turned to look at her. 'I have decided to return to England the day after tomorrow,' he told her abruptly.

Templar frowned. 'It's a bit short notice, Leon. It doesn't give me much time to get our things together.'

He bent to pick up the baby's plastic squeezy toy before answering her, dressed casually this morning in brown trousers and a fitted cream shirt. He looked lean and attractive and very self-assured, and their conversation of last night might never have taken place.

He looked at her coolly. 'I said *I* would be returning. The arrangements were for us to stay a couple of weeks, I see no reason for you not to stay that length of time, longer if you wish to.'

'But I—You intend returning without us?'

'That was my intention.' He picked up the toy again, giving Keri a mock stern look. 'I will take this away, young lady, if you do not stop throwing it about the room.'

Keri's answer was to toss it on to the floor again, laughing happily as her 'Dadda' returned it to her. 'Ta,' she gurgled.

Templar couldn't help smiling at the charm this child could exert over Leon, causing a softening to his normally harsh features as he too smiled at her.

'You don't want us to come with you?' she asked him.

He shook his dark head. 'It does not seem necessary. You may as well stay here with Keri.'

'But you—The day after tomorrow?' she queried sharply, a sudden thought occurring to her.

'That is correct.'

'I see,' she said tightly.

Leon's eyes narrowed as he looked at her. 'What do you see?'

She gave a harsh laugh. 'I see your reason for going back to England. Oh, Leon, you're so transparent! Rachel's leaving that day too, Neil told me that. So much for your denials about the two of you. I thought you an honest man, if a harsh one.'

'Thank you for that at least,' he replied tersely. 'And I had no idea when Rachel was leaving.'

'I don't believe you.'

'You may believe what you choose. I know for myself what is correct.'

'Why do you have to deny it? Can't you even admit it? I don't really have the right to object, so it won't make any difference to me.'

'I am sure it would not. But it is not true, and even to alleviate your own guilt I will not admit to something that is not so.'

'I don't feel guilty,' she denied hotly.

'Then perhaps you should. Do you not realise how stupid you have been, how dangerously stupid you have been towards me? Men do not consider things logically, the senses have more control over men than logic.'

'I thought you were always controlled,' she reminded him.

'Not with you, and I am not ashamed to admit it,' he said grimly. 'And when the time comes and that control gets out of hand you will find it very hard to stop me taking what I consider to be mine.'

'You—you wouldn't!' she gasped, realising that her lies of last night might have been in vain.

He stood up in preparation to leave. 'But I will, Templar. So be warned.'

She watched in dismay as he left the room, her shoulders slumping dejectedly. She had spent a restless night, her longing for Leon making it almost impossible for her to sleep. She had almost gone to his bedroom a couple of times during the night, had almost gone and offered herself to him. But in the end common sense had prevailed, making her realise that by doing that she would lose him.

She smiled vaguely at Keri as she banged the toy on her high-chair to attract her attention to her. 'All right, poppet. I haven't forgotten you. What shall we do this morning? The beach, or shall we go for a walk?' She chatted happily to Keri as she got her ready to go out, forcing her latest confrontation with Leon to the back of her mind.

The morning passed in relaxing pleasure with the baby, the beach proving as alluring as usual. She tried to forget her nervousness with Leon now, her fear of his threat towards her. But excitement kept invading her thoughts too and she just wanted to forget him.

Leon returned to the villa shortly before lunchtime, going upstairs to change in preparation for going out. He looked so self-assured and handsome, his dark skin shown to advantage against his snowy white trousers and shirt.

He quirked an eyebrow at her sitting figure. 'You are ready to go out?' he asked coolly.

She stood up, smoothing down the pale green skirt that matched her blouse. 'Yes, I'm ready.'

He nodded distantly. 'Then we will go.'

Neil Adams' villa seemed as crowded as it had

yesterday, maybe even more so, several of the people there not known to Templar. Leon left her side almost as soon as they came in, crossing the room to be at Rachel's side. Templar felt rather lost for several long minutes.

'And how are you today?' Neil was standing beside her, holding out a long cool drink of Bacardi and Coke.

She took the drink gratefully, conscious that Leon had noted the two of them talking together, scowling deeply before turning away again. 'I'm fine,' she smiled at him.

Neil watched her closely, gently touching the dark shadows that had started to appear under her eyes the last couple of days. 'Your beautiful face tells another story. Don't try to lie to me about your mood, Templar. Faces are my business, and I can tell just by looking at you how unhappy you are.'

'I'm trying not to think about it.'

'You can't stay with Leon just because of your child!' he said hotly. 'It will scar you in the end, and you aren't helping Keri at all. Believe me, I should know. I'm a product of one of these "we stayed together for the children" marriages. My mother couldn't stand my father and he felt the same way about her, but they had two children, my sister and myself, and they believed they had to stay together to give us a stable background.' He gave a bitter laugh. 'How ironic that is! I grew up hating both of them and the rows they were always having and thought we knew nothing about. Children can sense these things. Keri will when she's older.'

'It isn't quite the same thing——'

He gave a derisive smile. 'People always think their case is different.'

'But it really is. You see we—we've never been in

love, so there's nothing to go bitter between us.'

'You married because of Keri?' he guessed.

She couldn't look at him. 'Yes. We've only been married two months,' she admitted blushingly.

'I gather the baby was a mistake made in one of Leon's more reckless moments,' he said dryly, implying that he never realised Leon had such moments.

'Something like that,' she evaded.

Neil whistled between his teeth. 'What a mess!'

'That's what I think,' she smiled wanly.

'But he isn't having an affair with Rachel,' Neil added.

Templar looked at him sharply. 'How do you know that?'

'Because I asked her.'

'You—you asked her? And she told you, just like that?' She looked astounded.

'No, not just like that.' He looked slightly uncomfortable. 'I—er—I told her that I was interested in starting an affair with you and that I wanted to know where Leon stood.'

Templar gasped, 'You didn't!'

'I did, and it worked. She told me to wait a few days, that she was still working on him, that she was even considering staying on here after Wednesday in the hope of capturing him.'

So Leon had been telling the truth when he said he wasn't going back to England to be with Rachel; in that she had misjudged him. Perhaps she had misjudged him in other things too.

'I think we'll go in to lunch now,' Neil suggested. 'I hope you'll sit next to me?'

'Leon won't like it.'

'Oh, damn Leon! If you weren't married with that adorable baby I would take you away from him here and now. He doesn't deserve someone as beautiful as you.'

As she had known it would be, Leon's face was disapproving as she was seated next to Neil, Rachel at his other side, and Leon next to her. The meal passed with jokes and laughter all around them, a curious stillness about the four of them, despite Neil's attempts at conversation. By the time they reached the coffee stage of the meal Leon's anger was a tangible thing.

Finally his cup clattered down into the saucer. 'I am flattered, Neil, that you find my wife so fascinating that you cannot take your eyes off her,' he remarked tautly. 'But I am sure you are only making Templar feel uncomfortable.'

The whole room fell into tense silence at his barely controlled anger, everyone glancing at him uncertainly. Templar felt her gaze riveted to his harsh features as he glared challengingly at Neil.

Neil seemed unconcerned, still looking at her. 'I find your wife not only fascinating, Leon, but beautiful,' he said casually. 'But that isn't why I was staring at her. There's something about Templar that I find strangely familiar, something about her facial shape and the way she tilts her head to one side.'

Leon gave that mocking smile of his. 'Really?'

Conversation seemed to be flowing again, but Templar thought that most of the other diners were still half-listening to the veiled argument going on between the two men.

'Mm,' Neil looked thoughtful. 'I think it's another model. The colouring's different, of course, but there's definitely something . . .'

'You must mean Tiffany,' Rachel remarked disinterestedly, losing interest now that the argument seemed to be fading.

Templar looked away from Leon's searching gaze, pretending an interest in her half-cold coffee.

'I do?' Neil looked puzzled. 'Yes, I do,' he agreed. 'You look like that model Tiffany. I remember she died a little while ago—you took her place on that assignment, Rachel. How did you know I meant her?' he asked her.

'Well, it had to be her. She——'

'But we're nothing alike,' interrupted Templar quickly, although she thought it was too late now to stop the truth coming out. 'Tiffany was blonde-haired and blue-eyed, nothing at all like me.'

'But she was, Templar,' Neil persisted. 'Don't forget, I make a study of faces, bone structure and all that. It was definitely her.'

'Of course it was.' Rachel looked bored by the whole conversation.

Neil was irritated by her attitude. 'Stop being so damned smug, Rachel. Why should you be so certain about it?'

'Because they were sisters, silly.' She laughed at his expression. 'Didn't you know that?'

Templar was no longer listening to them but was watching Leon's reaction to this disclosure. His eyes were on her too, filled with contemptuous dislike, anger in every line of his body. She blamed herself for letting this happen. She should have realised that seeing Rachel like this would get her into trouble, that sooner or later the other girl would reveal things that Templar didn't want Leon to know.

And it was obvious from Leon's expression that she wouldn't be able to talk herself out of this one. That Tiffany was her sister was irrefutable, and she had the idea that Leon would demand a few answers to a few pertinent questions when they returned to their villa, like when exactly had Tiffany died, and why.

At the moment to ask such questions would be embarrassing to both of them, but she had no doubt he would do so once they were alone together. And she wasn't sure how she could answer him!

CHAPTER NINE

LEON paced up and down the lounge, glancing at her from time to time as if he were trying to puzzle her out. He shook his head. 'Why did you keep such a thing from me?'

She had known for the last two hours that this conversation was going to take place, and yet she was no nearer to finding him answers than she had been when Rachel had dropped that bombshell. She licked her lips. 'I don't know,' she replied huskily.

'You must have known how it would make me feel to know that you are the sister of the girl my brother wanted to marry. Why did you marry me, Templar— out of revenge for what I had done to your sister?' he asked darkly.

'No, I—Maybe I did think your family owed us something,' she admitted. 'Tiffany died because she loved your brother.'

'And you had my brother's child. Did you not want revenge for that too?'

'Perhaps,' she said stiffly.

'Tell me what it was like, to know that you were having the child of the man your sister loved.' There was cruelty in his look as if he were enjoying tormenting her.

'Please, Leon.' She stood up. 'Someone may come in, and Keri will be waking from her nap shortly. I have to go to her.'

'Like the doting mother that you are,' he scorned. 'Keri can wait a few moments. This conversation is far

from over. I have a few other things to ask you that
have been puzzling me.'

'I have to go, Leon,' she pleaded desperately.

'You will sit down and answer my questions! How
did your sister feel about the baby? Did she know it
was Alex's child you carried?'

'Yes, she knew,' Templar told him dully, having the
feeling that her whole world was about to crumble
about her ears. She was no good at lying and she knew
by the determination on Leon's face that he would
demand answers to all his questions, answers that could
only result in her own destruction.

'You told her this, even though you knew she loved
him?'

'I didn't need to tell her.'

'No,' he snapped, 'I am sure you did not. How could
you do that to her, to make her suffer the humiliation
of seeing you bear her lover's child?'

'I didn't do that! I—I loved Tiffany very much. I
would never have hurt her in any way.'

'No,' he sighed, 'I am beginning to believe you would
not. But you have enjoyed hurting me, have you not?
Last night——'

'I want to forget last night,' she interrupted sharply.
'It's over and done with.'

Leon flexed his tired shoulder muscles. 'It is far from
over. Something you said to me last night has been
bothering me. You could not bear me to be the substitute for my brother,' he said slowly. 'Because my dark
looks remind you of him, hmm?'

Templar looked away, aware that she wanted him
even now, that she longed to go to him and smooth
away the frown from between his eyes, to kiss and be
kissed by him until they could think of nothing but

each other. 'Yes,' she murmured finally, afraid to lift her eyes in case he should read her longings in their clear depths.

He drew in a deep breath. 'I see. Please wait here, Templar. I have something to show you.'

'I—I have to see to the baby.'

'You will wait here!' This time it was a command.

Within seconds he was back down the stairs, thrusting a photograph in front of her face. Templar put her hand out jerkily to take it, feeling a knife turn in her heart as she did so. It was a picture of Tiffany and a young man, a smiling happy Tiffany looking up adoringly at the man at her side.

She looked up at Leon imploringly. 'What do you want me to say?'

'That is your sister, is it not?'

'Yes.' She looked down again at the glowing face.

'And the young man with her?'

Templar shrugged. 'How should I know?' He was tall and blond, his brown eyes twinkling merrily as if the two in the photograph shared a secret joke. He was very handsome, tall, and smartly dressed in a cream lightweight suit. She put down the photograph. 'Don't tell me you had Tiffany followed too, to try and get evidence against her to blacken her name in your brother's eyes?'

'No, I did not do that. My brother worshipped your sister.' He picked up the photograph again. 'So you do not know this man?'

'Is it important? Surely it can't matter to Alex now he's dead?'

'It matters to me,' he said fiercely.

'So you're still trying to find reason to hate Tiffany, even though she can no longer hurt you.'

'No, I am not trying to do that. You see, the fact that you have lied to me about Tiffany being your sister——'

'I didn't lie. She *was* also a friend.'

'That is beside the point. You could so easily have told me of your relationship—but you chose not to. I asked myself why this was. Then I began to realise that if you had lied to me about one thing, then you could lie to me about others. Last night you said I reminded you of Alex, and I must admit to being slightly puzzled at the time. But I was in no mood to fathom the workings of a woman's mind just then. But today I have thought about it a lot, and you have just confirmed my conclusions. You never met my brother, did you?'

'How can you say that! Keri——'

'Is undoubtedly Alex's child, but she is certainly not yours. You see, the man in the photograph is my brother Alex. And you did not even recognise him!'

Templar paled, snatching the photograph out of his hand to stare down fixedly at the laughing boyish face. This couldn't be Alex Marcose! How could he have that startling blond hair and those laughing brown eyes? She became suddenly still, noting a certain similarity in the facial features between Leon and his brother, a certain arrogance in the stance that both men possessed.

'Oh, God!' she sighed chokingly.

'So the child, if she is not yours, must logically have been Tiffany's.'

'Yes.'

'And as Tiffany died a year ago I believe it also logical to assume she died almost immediately after giving birth to Keri.'

'Two hours later,' she confirmed.

Now it was his turn to pale. 'God, how you must hate

me for what I did to them! And for what I have done to you. If I had known of these facts we would not have been married, and you would not have had to put up with my insults.'

'You would have taken Keri away from me?'

He nodded. 'It is only right that she should be with me.'

'So now you know why I kept quiet. I didn't intend deceiving you about her, but your attitude when we first met pointed to you taking her away from me if you knew I was only her aunt. And I couldn't have allowed that to happen.'

'I do not understand your need to give up your own life for the sake of a baby I would gladly have allowed you free access to. As her aunt you would have the right to see her.'

Templar sighed. 'You'll never understand, will you, Leon? A woman doesn't automatically become a baby's mother at the birth of her child, in fact some women reject their babies at this stage. But nature provided for that by making it possible for another woman to love that child as if it were her own, as I love Keri. I don't have to be her real mother to feel excited at her first words, anguish over the cutting of her first teeth.'

He sighed.

'I was wrong to deny Alex the love he wanted from Tiffany, wrong to interfere,' he admitted.

'She never blamed anyone, Leon,' Templar assured him.

'I am sure she did not. She appears to have been a beautiful girl with an equally beautiful nature.'

'She was.'

'And you consider me responsible for both their deaths.'

'That isn't true,' she denied. 'You had allowed Alex

to go to her. You can't be held responsible for the accident that occurred after that.'

'Perhaps not, they said that the other driver was on the wrong side of the road. But he was not the one who was killed, my brother was!'

Templar better understood his determination to have Keri, could understand his need to have the one part of his brother that had survived. 'It's over now, Leon,' she comforted him. 'The past can't be undone.'

'That is true. But now we have our future to get through. What will happen, I wonder?'

'I don't understand what you mean?' She couldn't meet his piercing blue eyes.

'You must know very well what I mean. I am confused, utterly confused. I had formed my opinion of you, believed I knew what sort of person you are. Now I am unsure. I have to go and think this thing out.' He sounded preoccupied.

'What will happen to us?' she asked the question that was bothering her the most. His disclosure of today had changed the whole basis of their marriage. Their marriage had been based on what Leon believed about her, and now she had shattered all that. No wonder he was confused—she was confused herself.

'I do not know what will happen, that is what I must think out. I will return later.' He left so abruptly he took her by surprise.

Templar was left feeling utterly deflated. Her whole world seemed to be falling about her. Leon had reacted differently from how she had expected him to do. He had been angry, maybe a little shocked, but he hadn't ranted and raved as she had thought he would.

Maybe because she felt that this afternoon would be the deciding point in her life she spent the rest of Keri's waking time with her, not even wanting to leave her when she was fast asleep in her cot. But Marie had come up to tell her that Neil was downstairs waiting to see her, and so she straightened her hair and freshened her make-up before going downstairs.

'Hello, beautiful,' he came forward to kiss her on the cheek.

Templar's hands fidgeted together nervously. If Leon should come back and find Neil here ... 'Would —would you like a drink?' she offered politely.

He shook his head, watching her closely. 'Not just now, thanks. But you could invite me to dinner instead.'

'Oh, but——' her look was apprehensive.

'You don't have to worry about Leon,' he interpreted her look. 'He was over at my place when I left just now. Rachel was persuading him to stay for dinner.'

Her mouth tightened. 'Oh well, in that case ... Would you like to stay?'

'You know I would. I want to talk to you, maybe apologise for the trouble I probably got you into this afternoon. Was Leon very annoyed when you got home?' He sat down in the armchair as she became seated.

'Why should you think he was annoyed?' She avoided looking at him.

'I don't think it, I know it. I expected to see you black and blue this evening. His anger doesn't seem to have dispelled, in fact when I left just now he was drinking rather heavily.'

Her head snapped back. 'I can't believe Leon would ever be drunk! He has too much self-control to ever be seen like that.'

'Oh, he wasn't drunk,' Neil grinned. 'Just drinking as if the whisky was water. Rachel was revelling in his attention.'

'I'm sure she was. So you thought you would come over here and keep me company.'

'Something like that,' he admitted.

Templar couldn't feel any anger in the face of his friendly grin. 'Well, it was very nice of you to think of me. You're sure Leon won't be returning just yet?'

'What do you think?'

She sighed. 'I think you're probably right. I should think he's trying to forget I even exist at the moment.' She straightened. 'Never mind that for now. What did you want to talk to me about?'

'I wanted to know if you'd changed your mind about coming back to modelling?' He relaxed back in his chair.

'I told you, Leon wouldn't like it.'

'Oh, damn Leon! If he didn't exist would you go back? I have some assignments for you straight away if you'll consider it. Do you want them?'

'I can't answer that at the moment. I left modelling so that I could look after Keri and spend the time with her I thought she deserved. Now I'm thoroughly confused. I love Keri, but I don't feel she needs me any more. I feel superfluous.'

'You're not just Keri's mother, you're also Leon's wife—but are you?' His eyes narrowed with the sharpness of his question. 'I told you that it's my job to make a study of faces, and yours is very revealing. I don't believe you're Leon's wife, let alone the baby's mother,' he stated bluntly.

Templar attempted a light laugh. 'Don't be silly, Neil. Of course I'm married to Leon.'

'That isn't what I said.' His eyes softened with understanding. 'You may be married to Leon, but you certainly aren't his wife in the fullest sense.'

She gasped. 'How can you say that! Keri——'

'Is not your child,' he finished firmly. 'The eyes of a woman can be very expressive, and yours are totally innocent. You've never belonged to a man, let alone had a baby.'

'Don't be ridiculous, Neil!' she tried to pretend anger. 'I think you must have been the one that's had too much to drink, not Leon. I don't know where you get these ideas from, but they aren't——'

'*Are* true,' he interrupted. 'I know I keep going on about my knowledge of faces, but it's a fact that a lot can be read from them. Leon was as surprised as I was to find out Tiffany was your sister. Oh, he tried to hide it, but he wasn't quick enough. So after the two of you left I did a little detective work.'

'And came up with the wrong answers,' she scorned. Today was turning out to be a complete disaster, first Leon discovering her secret and now Neil. What else could possibly go wrong?

'The right ones,' he rebuked gently, breaking off as Marie came to tell them dinner was ready.

Sitting down to dinner and the serving of the food gave Templar a chance to collect her thoughts together, but it seemed that so much had happened today that nothing made sense any more. She felt lost and utterly defenceless, as if between the two of them Leon and Neil had stripped her soul bare.

She picked aimlessly at her food, not really wanting it, but Marie's constant trips in and out of the dining-room were making it impossible for Neil to pursue his line of conversation. But she knew he hadn't given up, knew it by the firm set of his mouth, knew that in some things he could be as adamant as Leon.

She smiled gratefully at Marie as she brought a tray of coffee into the lounge, the double doors opened out to the sea in the heat of the evening. It was curiously peaceful listening to the gentle lapping of the sea on the sand, and she felt herself begin to relax. After all, Neil was a friend, he wasn't about to condemn her behaviour.

'Feeling better?' He watched her over the rim of his coffee cup.

'Much better, thank you.' She didn't attempt to deny her former turmoil.

'Was my detective work correct?'

She shrugged. 'That really depends on what it told you.'

'It told me that Tiffany was Keri's mother and Leon's brother Alex the father. You somehow managed to convince Leon otherwise, that you were the mother. I think I can guess the reason for that. But I think he's only just found out the truth. It must have come as quite a shock to him.'

There was no use prevaricating any more. She must be worse at this than she had realised. 'Not as much as I thought it would be. I've apparently made a couple of slip-ups that have made him slightly suspicious, but I don't think he had realised the extent of my deceit.'

'So that's why he's over at my place drinking as if there's no tomorrow?'

'Yes.'

'So what are you going to do now?'

'I have no idea, it all depends on what Leon decides. Now that he knows the truth I can't see him letting me stay.'

'And how will you feel about that?'

How would she feel about it! Once she would have been devastated at being parted from Keri, but now that she knew how much Leon loved and cared for the baby, and that he would allow her to visit Keri whenever she wanted to, the child wasn't her prime concern.

To be parted from Leon would now be the hardest thing to bear, to meet only as strangers, their only link Keri.

'Don't answer that,' Neil said softly. 'I can see how you would feel about it. But if it did actually come to that, what would you do?'

She was trying not to think about it at all. 'I don't know,' she answered truthfully. 'Get myself a job, I suppose. Try to build a new life for myself.'

'Look, Templar, I still want to do those photographs of you. You're the only person I could possibly use for them. If you're worried about having somewhere to stay you could always move into the villa with me until you found somewhere of your own.'

'*My* wife will not be moving in with you anywhere for any length of time,' rasped a deep angry voice.

The two of them turned guiltily to face Leon. He stood just inside the open french doors, having entered unnoticed by either of them. He had an angry flush to his dark arrogant features. He moved further into the room, a mocking smile creasing his face. His glance passed insolently over the two of them.

Templar was mesmerised. He didn't look like the Leon who had left here a few hours earlier. There was a certain rakishness to his expression, his hair windswept, his white shirt opened almost to his waist. He looked—he looked devilish!

'Leon!' She stood up shakily.

His gaze swung back to her. 'Yes—Leon. I doubt, by your conversation, that you were expecting me home just yet. You were perhaps hoping not to be disturbed for a while.'

Neil flushed angrily at the other man's contemptuous tone, feeling at a distinct disadvantage sitting down. He stood up slowly. 'It isn't what it seems, Leon,' he began.

Grey-blue eyes turned glacial. 'I am sure it is exactly what it seems,' he sneered.

'Now look, Marcose——'

'No—*you* look,' Leon said fiercely, taking a threatening step towards the younger man. 'I wish to be left alone with my wife. You will kindly leave my house so that this is possible.'

'I don't——'

'You will leave now while you are able to do so,' Leon interrupted curtly. 'I have asked you politely so far, but the next time I may not even bother to ask. You understand?'

Neil looked uncertain. 'Templar?'

She pushed her hair back nervously. 'I—— Perhaps it would be for the best, Neil.' She had never seen Leon in such a mood; he looked positively dangerous, and there was a certain glazed look to his eyes. Perhaps Neil was right and Leon had been drinking too much. There was certainly something wrong with him.

Grey eyes raked her before passing on to Neil. 'You heard my wife, Adams. Leave.'

'You're sure?' Neil looked at her worriedly.

'I'm sure,' she answered hurriedly as she saw Leon's look darken threateningly.

'So,' Leon mocked sneeringly once Neil had left. 'You are never at a loss for male company, are you? I am gone for a few hours and straight away you invite your lover over here. Unfortunately for you I noticed his absence at dinner.'

'Really?' Templar looked away. 'I'm surprised you noticed anything, the state you're in.'

His eyes flashed angrily. 'What do you mean?'

'I mean you're drunk!'

Leon gave a harsh laugh that owed nothing to amusement. 'I am not drunk. It takes more than a few whiskies to get me in that state.'

'You could have fooled me!' she retorted with more courage than she felt. 'And Neil is not my lover. He was just comforting me as a friend.'

'Oh yes? Do all your male friends invite you to go and live with them?'

'It wasn't meant that way and you know it!'

'I know only one thing, I will stand no more of it. I have come to the end of my patience where you are concerned.'

'Wh—what do you mean to do?' she faltered.

He gave a cruel smile. 'You may well ask. Do not look so nervous, Templar. You may enjoy the next couple of hours,' he gave a shrug, 'but it is not important that you do. Today I went to see Rachel Winter with the intention of accepting her blatant offer for me to share her bed,' his grin was even crueller at her gasp of dismay. 'Why so shocked? Is it not what you have always suspected of me?'

'Yes, but I——'

'Mm, well, today would have been the first time I have made love to a woman since we were married. And I would have taken her too—if I had not seen your face in my mind all the time!' He angrily slammed the french doors closed, locking them with a snap of the catch. 'I could feel nothing for her, nothing at all!'

'I—I see.' She bit her top lip.

'I do not really think that you do,' he said bitterly. 'You have made it impossible for me to make love to another woman, so you must be the one to satisfy me.'

Templar took a step back at the determination in his face. 'No!' she shook her head desperately.

'Oh yes. I will no longer be put off. The obstruction of Keri being your child has effectively been removed. There is no further reason why I should not have what many men have surely had before me.'

'Oh no, Leon,' she choked. 'You can't expect——'

His eyes narrowed and his mouth tightened. 'I expect you to go to your room and wait for me there!'

Her face paled. 'I can't, Leon!'

'You will do as you are told!' he snapped. 'I intend taking you if I have to fight you to do it. You will torment me no longer. Go to your room,' he repeated. 'I will come to you in ten minutes.'

She gave one last pleading look at his determined face before turning to leave the room. Leon would not be moved by emotion, he had gone past that. He was a man set on an idea and he wouldn't be deterred by anything.

'And, Templar ...' he halted her exit, 'do not imagine you can sneak out of the villa away from me. If you leave I will follow you and bring you back, no matter where you are. I intend ridding myself of this passion I have for you once and for all. Ten minutes,' he reminded her threateningly.

CHAPTER TEN

TEMPLAR sat down on the bed, tears racking her slender body. And she had thought nothing else could go wrong today! This was the worst of all. Leon intended taking her without thought of her feelings in the matter, without caring whether she wanted him in return.

Her shoulders slumped. But of course he knew she wanted him—she betrayed her desire for him every time he came near her. Yes, she wanted him, and he knew it. He also knew she had no choice but to give in to his demands.

Well, he wouldn't find her lying dejectedly in the bed waiting for him when he came in here. If tonight was to be her wedding night then she was going to look the part.

She found herself a sheer white nightdress, laying it on the bed before going to take a shower. She washed herself thoroughly before smoothing scented lotion all over her body. Back in her bedroom she donned the nightdress and brushed her hair smoothly. A spray of perfume, the lights dimmed to the two side-lamps, and she felt ready to face her husband.

She did not have long to wait, only a minute or two before he walked unannounced into the bedroom, his eyes narrowing as he took in the dimmed room and her body clothed in the sheer nightdress. Under that mocking stare Templar found she didn't feel quite so confident.

'So,' he said softly. 'You have decided to play the virgin for me.'

Templar flinched at the scorn in his voice but didn't retaliate. 'If you mean I've decided not to fight you then you're right,' she agreed softly. 'What would be the point?'

'Admit you do not want to fight me.' He slowly removed his robe, revealing the only other garment he wore, a pair of cream silk pyjama trousers that rested low on his hip bones and emphasised the darkness of his skin.

'I have no choice,' she replied obstinately.

'No, you do not. Take off that ridiculous nightdress and get into bed. Did you expect me to feel remorse with you in virginal white?' he scoffed. 'What a mockery that is! You have no right to wear the colour, no right at all.'

Colour flared in her pale cheeks. 'I have the right of a bride on her wedding night!'

He gave that harsh laugh that was wholly taunting. 'You do not have the right when another man has already taken the virginity that colour is supposed to imply. Now take it off and get into bed!' he ordered.

Templar felt her courage begin to fail her at the callousness in his face. 'I can't do it, Leon. Not like this. Please, don't take me like this!' she begged him, her green eyes imploring.

'I will take you any way I choose. I see no reason for you to enjoy it. Now will you take that thing off or do I have to rip it from your body?'

'Like you did the last time?' she scorned.

'Exactly as I did the last time, although this time you will not escape so easily.' He sat down in the bedroom chair, his eyes never leaving her body.

She felt herself blushing under his intent stare. 'I can't do it with you looking at me.'

'Well, I have no intention of turning the other way.'

She set her lips, pulling the nightdress up over her head, her naked body bathed in golden light from the side-lamps. 'Are you satisfied now?'

'Hardly,' he said dryly. 'I will not be that until you are in bed and I have made you mine.' He stood up and she moved hurriedly beneath the covers, but she needn't have panicked so quickly, he was merely standing up to remove his pyjama trousers. She looked away from his muscled god-like body, blushing profusely.

Leon came to stand beside the bed, looking down at her pale face. 'Perhaps I will make it pleasurable for you after all,' he mused softly, pulling back the sheet to reveal her naked body. 'To merely take you is not enough. I want you to beg for my possession of you. Yes,' he gave that cruel smile again, 'I will make you beg.'

Templar felt herself tense as he lay beside her, the long length of his body pressed intimately close against her side. 'The lights, Leon. Turn out the lights.'

He leant over her, kissing her throat with caressing lips: 'I want them left on. I want to watch you as I make love to you, I want to see your every emotion.'

'Oh God, Leon!' she choked. 'Does it have to be a punishment?'

One strong hand moved up to cup one full breast, his mouth moving slowly over her shoulder and down to its fullness. 'You do not expect me to take you with love, do you? To treat you as a real wife?'

'No,' she shook her head from side to side, feeling her body begin to weaken towards him as his hand continued its exploration of her taut body. 'But I——'

'Be silent!' His tongue licked flames along her body. 'Before I have finished with you you will be saying something so much different.'

He pulled her roughly against him, turning her into

his arms so that their two bodies were moulded together. His mouth claimed hers, forcing her lips apart
and demanding she respond.

She didn't want to do anything else with his fully
aroused body pressed against her, his hands running
caressingly up and down her body from shoulder to
thigh. She shuddered as his hand claimed her breast,
his fingers experienced when it came to the workings of
a woman's body.

'Do you like that, Templar?' he whispered against
her parted mouth. 'Tell me you like it.'

'I—' she gasped as he touched her again. 'I like it,'
she admitted breathlessly.

'Good. Now touch me, Templar,' he ordered. 'Touch
me! Where is all the experience you are supposed to
have? Do you not know how to caress and please a
man?'

'I know nothing of men. Nothing!'

'Then I will show you!'

He forced her hands on to his body, showing her
how best to please him. Within minutes she felt dizzied
by his kisses, almost dreamlike with the feelings he was
arousing in her body. That he was an expert was obvious and she couldn't hold back her gasps of pleasure
and her own fevered caresses.

His was the only male body she had ever touched
and she found him beautiful. That he found her
equally desirable was obvious, and their mouths met
and clung, met and clung, and Templar knew this
could be the wedding night she had always dreamt of.

At his insistent caresses of her breasts she felt a
tension start to rise up within her, a feeling of tension
that demanded release. That Leon was aware of these
feelings she had no doubt, but he still continued those

soul-destroying kisses, one of his legs pinning her to the bed.

His face buried in her throat, he licked flames of fire along her skin, moaning his pleasure at her own caressing hands. 'Oh, God,' he breathed deeply, shuddering. 'I cannot stand much more,' he groaned. 'Ask me to take you, Templar. Beg me.'

'Oh yes, yes! Take me, Leon,' she pleaded. 'I want you to take me.'

'Beg!'

'I'm begging you, Leon. I'm begging you!'

She didn't even notice the weight of his body, not even in control of herself any more. She felt weightless, as if she were flying high on a cloud. His touch was gentle now, not punishing any longer as his own longing took over and he could no longer think of anything but the beautiful body beneath him.

His mouth on hers could not wholly smother her cry of pain and he drew back, his face white with disbelief. He looked dazed. 'It cannot be,' he muttered. 'It cannot be,' he groaned.

The first initial pain had faded now and she moved against him longingly, willing him on now that she was completely roused and mindless. Her movements were all he needed to lose control again and their passions mounted high until they burst in a flash of rainbow-coloured lights and a feeling of such intense relief that Templar felt faint.

'That was beautiful, Leon,' she murmured sleepily. 'Just beautiful.'

He moved away from her, his face still deathly white and his thoughts confused. 'You were untouched,' he stated bluntly.

Templar turned to kiss his shoulder, frowning as she

felt him flinch. 'Does it matter?' she asked softly.

For answer he pulled out of her questing arms and stood up, swaying slightly in the aftermath of passion. He ran a hand through his ruffled hair, looking down at her with tortured eyes before hurriedly covering her naked body with the sheet. 'I have never ever violated the body of an innocent!'

She felt strangely like laughing at his grim expression, lightheaded, her body languidly replete. Tonight she had become a woman in his arms, and it had been wonderful. 'Come back to bed, Leon. We'll talk in the morning.'

'We most certainly will,' he said with suppressed violence. 'You will want to return immediately to England, I understand that.'

'I will?' she frowned.

'Yes, I—— Oh God, I am so sorry! Why did you not tell me?' he demanded.

'Would it have made any difference? You wouldn't have believed me.'

'No, I would not.' He threw on his robe. 'There is no way I can make up to you what I have just done, no way I can undo it. But I will try, I will surely try.'

'How?'

'I will give you anything you want. I will buy you a house anywhere you want to live. I will pay you a large allowance,' he promised heatedly.

It seemed he would give her everything but the one thing she really wanted, and that was to stay with him. 'You want me to go?' she faltered.

'You must see it is impossible for us to carry on living together as we have been. It could no longer work.'

Templar didn't see anything of the sort, but that Leon wanted her out of his life was obvious. He couldn't have felt the same way she did about their lovemaking. To him it had been a violation of an innocent body, not the beautiful experience she considered it to be.

That she owed much of her enjoyment to Leon's experience she had no doubt. He knew exactly what to do to induce the right pleasures at the right time, and even though he wanted to forget it had ever happened she wanted to remember it for ever. It would probably be the only time she would ever know such delights. She knew she would never want any other man but Leon, and he no longer seemed to want her.

'Why wouldn't it?' she asked huskily.

'Because I can no longer bear to have you near me!'

He wasn't looking at her, so he didn't see her flinch. 'All right,' she sighed her defeat. 'I'll get out of your life as soon as I can.'

'There is no rush. We will have to talk in the morning. I cannot think straight at the moment.' He glanced at her fleetingly. 'Try to rest now and perhaps sleep will dull the memory of what I have just done to you.'

'Leon, I——'

'Please, do not say another word.' He wrenched open the door. 'We must both sleep on this. See how we feel in the morning,' he gave a grim smile. 'I have never met anyone like you for throwing me into a state of utter confusion.'

'No, Leon.' Tears shimmered in her deep green eyes.

'And, Templar . . .' he turned to look at her, 'I am sorry.'

She shook her head. 'Please don't . . .'

'You are right,' he braced his shoulders. 'What I have done cannot be erased with an apology.' He quietly closed the door as he left.

Templar turned over, burying her face in the pillows. She didn't want the memory erased, she wanted to remember and remember. Why couldn't Leon have felt the same elation and joy she had felt? To him she had been no different from any of the other women he had taken and then discarded. And that was the reason she had to leave.

She didn't want to be someone he made love to when in the mood, someone he turned to when frustration overtook him. If she couldn't be the one woman he loved then she didn't want to be anything in his life. She would leave now, get a flight to England and be back there before he even realised she had gone.

It was early yet, only just ten o'clock, and a quick telephone call to the airport confirmed that there was a seat for her on the one o'clock flight. She got out of bed, moving with renewed vigour. It would be better this way, to take herself far away from Leon, far away from the temptation to be in his arms.

She spent fifteen minutes with Keri, not knowing when she would see the baby again but hoping Leon would allow it to be soon. She could probably stay with Mary and Peter for a couple of days until she found somewhere of her own. One thing was certain, she wasn't going to live off Leon. She would find herself a job, perhaps go back to modelling and support herself.

The one problem now seemed to be transport to the airport. Ten-thirty. Neil would probably be far from going to bed yet, and she thought he might like to help her.

If he thought it strange to meet her in ten minutes outside the villa he didn't ask any questions on the telephone, although she knew he would be more curious when they actually met.

He raised a questioning eyebrow at her packed suitcase, silently stowing it in the boot of the car. 'The airport?' He put the car into gear.

'If you wouldn't mind.'

'I don't mind at all,' he smiled at her. 'I'm only glad you turned to me for help.'

'I had no one else,' she answered truthfully.

'I can understand that. You have that look in your eyes now,' he said suddenly.

Templar blushed. 'I don't know what you mean.'

'Yes, you do. Is that why you're leaving?'

'Yes,' she told him shortly. What was the use of arguing with him? He was much too observant to be taken in by anything she said to the contrary.

'It was my fault, wasn't it?' said Neil. 'He was angry at finding us together.'

'He was angry, yes. But that wasn't the reason he—well, that wasn't why it happened.'

'But the baby, how do you feel about leaving her?'

'How do you think I feel?' She choked over the words, her tears starting again. Keri had looked so beautiful, tucked up in her cot. It had been a wrench leaving her behind, but she knew that Leon would only come after her if she took Keri away from him. He loved the baby very much even if he didn't love her.

Neil put a comforting hand over hers. 'I'm sorry, Templar. You must feel like hell.'

'Yes,' she agreed.

Neil slowed the car down, pulling it on to the side of the road and turning off the ignition. 'Are you sure you're doing the right thing by leaving?'

'What else can I do?' she sighed defeatedly.

'You could try staying and fighting for what you want,' he suggested gently.

'I don't know what I want any more. Not after to-night . . .' she trailed off miserably.

Neil put his arm about her shoulders. 'I would have thought tonight would have told you a lot.'

'Like what?'

'Like Leon finds you very attractive, that he desires you. Isn't that enough to be going on with?'

She shook her head. 'It isn't enough.'

'You want him to love you too, hmm?'

Her head shot up and she looked at him in the darkness. 'Why do you say that?' she quavered.

'Because all these tears aren't just for the baby. You love Leon, don't you?'

'There's no point in denying it,' she said dully. 'Yes, I love him. But he doesn't love me.'

'How do you know that?'

She gave a harsh laugh. 'It's obvious, I would have thought. Doesn't your knowledge of faces tell you that just by looking at him?'

'Leon's face isn't quite so easily read. He's a very hard man to fathom. But I would say that he's more possessive over you than any other woman he's ever had in his life. You puzzle him. I've seen him looking at you, as if he can't make his mind up about you.'

'That was before. He knows everything about me now.' Much more than he had bargained for!

'Mm, perhaps. But I think he's the sort of man who will love only once in his life, and when he does it will be for ever.'

She sighed. 'Perhaps—but it won't be me he loves.'

'You could be wrong——' he broke off, turning in his seat to look out of the back window. 'In fact I'm sure you are. A car has just stopped behind us and at a guess I would say it was Leon.'

'Leon! But——' she too turned, just in time to see her door wrenched open and the blazingly angry face of her husband thrust inside the car.

'It seems that once again I have to ask you to leave my wife alone,' he snapped contemptuously.

'Leon, it isn't like that!'

'Explanations can wait until we return home,' he told her shortly. 'You will please get into our car.'

'Leon, please let me explain,' she pleaded.

'You will explain nothing,' he helped her out of Neil's car. 'You will wait for me in the car.'

Templar looked at Neil, shrugging. 'I'm sorry about this.'

'Do as Leon wants, Templar,' he advised gently. 'It's for the best.'

Within a few minutes Leon had joined her in the car, putting her cases in the back, his expression not quite so grim. 'You weren't rude to him?'

'I have done nothing except tell your friend that in future I will allow you to be alone with no man but me.'

'I was leaving you, Leon.' She held her head high. 'Taking me back to the villa won't change that. I'll just get another flight tomorrow.'

'You will not get a flight from me tomorrow or any other time,' he declared calmly. 'I will not allow it.'

'Don't you think it would have been best to let me go? This way you're just prolonging the agony.'

'Agony!' he ground out fiercely. 'What do you think I have been suffering for the last hour? And when I came back to find you gone ...'

Templar frowned. 'I didn't even realise you had gone out.'

'Yes,' he said shortly. 'I went for a long walk on the beach to try and clear my head. I wanted to think.' He stopped the car outside the villa, coming round to open her door for her.

Her body came up close against his as she stepped out, making her very much aware of how attractive he looked in the clinging black shirt and the fitted black trousers. She dragged her gaze away and walked into the villa.

She turned to face him as they came into the lounge, feeling herself defeated already by his attractiveness. God, how she loved him! 'What was the point of bringing me back here? It only means I'll have to say goodbye all over again.'

'You did not say goodbye to me a first time!'

'I didn't see the need. You had already told me you were going to send me away.'

'But not like that! To sneak off into the night without telling me you were leaving. And I do not for one moment suppose you were going to tell me where you were going to live.'

'I—I would have done eventually. I would have wanted to see Keri. You told me I could have free access to her,' she added pleadingly.

'Oh, Templar,' he shook his head. 'What sort of monster do you think I am? I would not take your child away from you.'

'But she—she isn't . . .' she blushed.

'She is your child in every way that matters.' His eyes were startlingly blue against the darkness of his skin. 'I admit that at first I would have taken her away without a qualm. But not now, not now I have seen how you love her. No, Templar, it is not for you to prove your right to be her mother, it is up to me to prove I am fit to be her father. So far I do not seem to have been a very good husband or father.'

'That isn't true. Keri loves you.'

'And you, how do you feel about me?' he gave a harsh laugh. 'Do not answer that. I can imagine your feelings towards me.'

'Then why bring me back here? Why couldn't you

just let me go quietly out of your life?'

His face was pale in the lamplight, his expression grim. 'If you go out of my life, now or at any other time, it could not be done quietly.'

Templar smoothed her warm hands down her trouser-clad thighs. 'But you said you wanted me to go, to live apart from you.'

'But not like this, and not for ever. I wanted you to live apart from me so that you could get to know the real me, get to know the person I am.'

She didn't understand him. 'But I can get to know you here.'

'No, you cannot,' he said tautly, pouring himself a large amount of whisky into a glass and drinking it in one gulp. 'I—— When you are near me I can think only of making love to you. I was like an animal this evening! I took you with no thought of—of anything but myself. You cannot imagine the shock I felt when I found you to be untouched. I am so ashamed of what I did to you, of what I have done to us both.'

'But I—' she licked her lips. 'I liked what you did to me. I liked it, Leon!'

He didn't look at her. 'I am not so inexperienced where women are concerned that I did not know that. This is another reason it would be for the best if we lived apart. I do not want your emotions to be blinded by physical gratification. We are good in bed together. You know exactly how to please me, and I hope I please you. But this is not all I want from you. I want so much more.'

Hope flared within her. 'What do you want from me, Leon? What else can I give you?'

'I do not know if I can expect anything else. I have forced on you a relationship that can only have disgusted you.' The greyness increased about his mouth.

'I leave for England tomorrow. You can stay on here and when you return you will move back into the house with the baby. I will be the one to move out—until such time as perhaps——'

'Perhaps what, Leon?' she prompted desperately.

He slammed the glass down savagely on the coffee-table and came to stand in front of her. Templar was amazed at the look of uncertainty on his face. 'Until such time as perhaps you can take me back into your life.'

'But you don't have to leave it.'

Leon gently cupped either side of her face, his stern mouth curved into a smile. 'I can no longer be satisfied with the sort of relationship we have had. Even to-night, when I knew what I had taken from you, I wanted you again. I had to leave your bedroom before I could no longer control myself.'

So that was the reason for his abrupt departure from her room! And she had thought it was because she disgusted him, that he regretted what had happened between them. The deep look in his eyes seemed to be telling her something she found hard to believe, wanted to believe, but found she just couldn't.

'I wanted you to stay with me, Leon,' she whispered. 'I tried to ask you to stay, but you wouldn't let me.'

He looked impatient. 'You were blinded by what had just happened. I was your first lover, you are only natural in feeling a certain softening of feelings towards me. But I want more from you. I want your love, Templar.'

'But you already have it.' She trembled with the enormity of her declaration.

Leon shook his head sadly, his hands dropping to his sides. 'Not like this, Templar,' he said with a groan. 'I don't want it to be like this. For a long time now I have loved you. I have loved the gentleness of you, the softness of you. I love your body too, I cannot deny that, but it is not all I love. I love *you*, Templar, all of you.'

She couldn't believe she was hearing him correctly. Leon, cold, hard, often unfeeling Leon, loved *her*! Her face began to glow and she felt like crying with happiness. 'Oh, Leon,' she choked, 'I love you too.'

If anything his face became grimmer. 'You love what I have made you feel,' he contradicted gently.

'No, oh no!' She ran to stand in front of him, smoothing away the frown from between his eyes. She put her arms about his waist, resting her face on his rapidly rising and falling chest. 'I realised the other night when you came to my room for the first time that I loved you, but it had happened long before that. The time you brought Rachel to the house I was not only angry, I was jealous. Oh, Leon, I love you!'

She stood on tiptoe to kiss him on the mouth, moving against him and feeling him suddenly relax against her, his arms clamping about her like steel bands.

'I hope you mean this, Templar,' he groaned fiercely. 'Because I cannot let you go now. I cannot!' he repeated achingly.

He was literally shaking against her and she cried with her own happiness. 'I wouldn't let you send me away now. I wouldn't go even if you attempted to do it.'

His face softened with love, he bent his head to claim her lips in a kiss that began gently but soon deepened into consuming passion. They were hungry for each other, aware of each other's love now, their senses heightened to breaking point.

Leon pulled back, his breathing ragged with emotion. 'Thank God I came back from my walk when I did! I came to your room to see you, to tell you what I had decided, only to find you already gone. You can have no idea how I felt when I found some of your clothing gone,' he shuddered. 'And when I followed you only to find you had left with Neil Adams——! I felt like death, my darling.'

'I didn't leave with Neil,' she said, 'he was just giving me a lift to the airport.'

He rested his forehead against hers, his hands clasped together at the base of her spine, their two bodies moulded together. 'I have suffered agonies the last few days, imagining you to be in love with him. I could not have stood that.'

'He's been a friend, Leon, nothing more. He guessed the true circumstances of Keri's birth.'

He sighed. 'I wish to God I had! I could have saved myself so much torment. To imagine other men having made love to you has been absolute hell for me. I should have known, should have guessed. I have never known what it was to be so murderously jealous before. You are my first and only love, Templar.'

'And you mine,' she smiled shyly.

He gave a deep shuddering sigh. 'I have so longed to hear you say that, I can hardly believe it.'

'I feel the same. Leon, are you—will you be sharing my bed tonight?' Delicate colour flooded her cheeks.

His look was probing. 'Do you want me to?'

'So much,' she admitted huskily. 'So very much.'

He swung her up in his arms, bending to kiss her before kicking the door open and marching up the stairs with her still in his arms.

'Leon,' she giggled, 'someone may see us! What will they think?'

'I could not give a damn!' He gave a triumphant laugh. 'I love you and I do not care who knows it. And I do not care who knows I am about to make passionate

love to my wife into the early hours of the morning. I
do not care!'

Templar's eyes glowed her own satisfaction of such
an arrangement as she snuggled into his throat, eager
to give the rest of her nights and days into Leon's keeping.

The Mills & Boon Rose is the Rose of Romance

Look for the Mills & Boon Rose next month

PAGAN LOVER by *Anne Hampson*
Tara had been forced to marry the masterful Leon Petrides
and there was no escape — but did she really want to get away?

GARDEN OF THORNS by *Sally Wentworth*
Somebody was trying to get rid of Kirsty, but she just *couldn't*
believe it was the autocratic Squire, Gyles Grantham.

KELLY'S MAN by *Rosemary Carter*
Kelly found it very galling that, despite all her efforts, Nicholas
Van Mijden should still persist in thinking of her as just a
spoiled rich girl.

DEBT OF DISHONOUR by *Mary Wibberley*
Renata's job was to look after a difficult teenage girl — but she
found the girl's forbidding uncle more difficult and unpredict-
able to deal with!

CRESCENDO by *Charlotte Lamb*
'If you let them, women will take you over completely,' was
Gideon Firth's philosophy — and that philosophy had ruined
Marina's life.

BAY OF STARS by *Robyn Donald*
Bourne Kerwood had been described as 'a handsome bundle
of dynamite' — and that dynamite had exploded all over
Lorena's young life!

DARK ENCOUNTER by *Susanna Firth*
'For the salary you're offering I'd work for the devil himself'
— and when Kate started work for Nicholas Blake she soon
began to wonder if that wasn't just what she *was* doing . . .

MARRIAGE BY CAPTURE by *Margaret Rome*
Married against her will, Claire promised herself that the
marriage would be in name only — but that promise was a
surprisingly difficult one to keep!

BINDABURRA OUTSTATION by *Kerry Allyne*
'Go back to the city where you belong,' ordered Kelly Sinclair
contemptuously, and Paige would have been only too glad to
oblige — but fate forestalled her . . .

APOLLO'S DAUGHTER by *Rebecca Stratton*
Bethany resented Nikolas Meandis when he tried to order her
life for her — and that was before she realised just what he
was planning for her . . . .

If you have difficulty in obtaining any of these books from
your local paperback retailer, write to:

Mills & Boon Reader Service
P.O. Box 236, Thornton Road, Croydon, Surrey, CR9 3RU.

Available May 1980

SAVE TIME, TROUBLE & MONEY!
By joining the exciting NEW...

Mills & Boon 🌷

Romance CLUB

WITH all these EXCLUSIVE BENEFITS for every member

NOTHING TO PAY! MEMBERSHIP IS FREE TO REGULAR READERS!

IMAGINE the *pleasure* and *security* of having ALL your favourite *Mills & Boon* romantic fiction delivered right to *your* home, absolutely POST FREE... straight off the press! No waiting! No more disappointments! All this PLUS all the latest news of *new books* and *top-selling authors* in your own monthly MAGAZINE... PLUS *regular* big CASH SAVINGS... PLUS lots of wonderful strictly-limited, *members-only* SPECIAL OFFERS! All these exclusive benefits can be *yours* – right NOW – simply by joining the exciting NEW *Mills & Boon* ROMANCE CLUB. Complete and post the coupon below for FREE full-colour leaflet. It costs nothing. HURRY!

No obligation to join unless you wish!

FREE CLUB MAGAZINE Packed with *advance* news of latest titles and authors

Exciting offers of **FREE BOOKS** For club members ONLY

Lots of fabulous **BARGAIN OFFERS** —many at **BIG CASH SAVINGS**

FREE FULL-COLOUR LEAFLET!
CUT OUT *CUT-OUT COUPON BELOW AND POST IT TODAY!*

To: **MILLS & BOON READER SERVICE, P.O. Box No 236, Thornton Road, Croydon, Surrey CR9 3RU, England.**
WITHOUT OBLIGATION to join, please send me FREE details of the exciting NEW **Mills & Boon** ROMANCE CLUB and of all the exclusive benefits of membership.

Please write in BLOCK LETTERS below

NAME (Mrs/Miss) ....

ADDRESS ....

CITY/TOWN ....

COUNTY/COUNTRY.........................POST/ZIP CODE.........................

S. African & Rhodesian readers write to:
P.O. BOX 11190, JOHANNESBURG, 2000. S. AFRICA

Mills & Boon Classics

The very best of Mills & Boon
romances, brought back for those of
you who missed reading them
when they were first published.

in
April
we bring back the following four
great romantic titles.

CINDERELLA IN MINK
by Roberta Leigh

Nicola Rosten was used to the flattery and deference accorded
to a very wealthy woman. Yet Barnaby Grayson mistook her
for a down-and-out and set her to work in the kitchen!

MASTER OF SARAMANCA
by Mary Wibberley

Gavin Grant was arrogant and overbearing, thought Jane, and
she hadn't ever disliked anyone quite so much. Yet . . .

NO GENTLE POSSESSION
by Anne Mather

After seven years, Alexis Whitney was returning to Karen's
small town. It was possible that he might not even remember
her — but Karen hoped desperately that he did.

A SONG BEGINS
by Mary Burchell

When Anthea began her training with the celebrated operatic
conductor, Oscar Warrender, she felt her dreams were coming
true — but would she be tough enough to work under such an
exacting taskmaster?

If you have difficulty in obtaining any of these books through
al paperback retailer, write to:

Mills & Boon Reader Service
ton Road, Croydon, Surrey, CR9 3RU.